Behind the Mist

To Wyatt,
Have fun reading!

M. J. Evans

Behind the Mist

— BOOK ONE OF THE MIST TRILOGY —

M.J. Evans

Langdon Street Press
Minneapolis, MN

Langdon Street Press
212 3rd Avenue North, Suite 290
Minneapolis, MN 55401
612.455.2293
www.langdonstreetpress.com

ISBN-13: 978-1-936183-87-6
LCCN: 2010938775

Cover Design and Typeset by Sophie Chi

Printed in the United States of America

For my wonderful husband,
children, and grandchildren.
Without your encouragement,
this could never have been written.
And for my friends who enthusiastically
read every chapter.

"There is no fear in love;
But perfect love casteth out fear."

1 John 4:18 (KJV)

CONTENTS

chapter 1
Jazz

The dark head of the horse shot straight up in the air. The bit tore against the soft tissue at the corners of his mouth as the rider pulled on the reins, trying desperately to remain in the saddle. The mud and loose rocks carried them down the side of the cliff. For several feet, the horse was successful as he scrambled to keep upright; but eventually, the steep descent became too much for him and he started tumbling, carrying his rider with him.

Thunder echoed against the canyon walls, but was drowned out by the sound of the waterfall crashing against the boulders at the base. A cold plume of mist rose high into the air. The two bodies rolled and bounced down the side of the cliff. When they landed at the base of the falls, the horse's body was wedged between two sharp boulders. The rider was trapped underneath him, his face pressed against the stones beneath the surface of the water. The mist provided the burial shroud.

The waterfall parted like the curtain on a stage. A dapple-gray unicorn appeared from behind the mist and stepped out onto his rocky proscenium. His entire body sparkled like silver and his long horn shone as if it were a beam of light. The unicorn looked down at the dark horse with his soft, liquid eyes. "Come with me, Jazz," the glorious creature said kindly.

"I cannot. I cannot leave my rider."

"Nicholas has his own path to follow."

"No, I will never leave him."

Five years earlier...

The jagged peaks of the Rocky Mountains stood out proudly several miles to the west as the Boeing 757 jet from Newark landed beside the white peaks on the plains that housed Denver International Airport. The curly-haired boy watched out the window and kept his eyes glued to the mountains more to settle his churning stomach from the typical rough Denver descent than for any other reason. He kept watching to the west as the plane touched down on the tarmac and taxied toward the B terminal.

Nick was twelve years old, and his family was leaving behind the hustle, bustle, and humidity of New York City for three months to live in a cabin on the eastern edge of Rocky Mountain National Park northwest of Denver, Colorado.

As the family drove up to Estes Park, Nick continued staring toward the ridge of mountains from the window of the van his parents rented for the summer. He had studied the formation of the Rocky Mountains in school. He remembered that they were created as the plates that make up the surface of the Earth shifted and collided with one another.

His eyes followed the tops of the mountains, from Long's Peak in the north and located in the park itself, to Mount Evans directly west of Denver. His eyes moved down the row of mountaintops to where Pike's Peak stood alone guarding over Colorado Springs. Nick gazed at the majestic peaks with admiration, thrilled to actually be seeing them. He was equally overwhelmed by the enormous sky. The sky did not look this big in New York City, even in Central Park.

Behind him, his two younger sisters released their excitement by giggling as they poked one another and, on occasion, him. He ignored them, content to savor the vast expanse of the plains as they gently rolled up to the magnificent mountains that would be their home for the summer.

When the van's tires ceased crunching on the gravel drive that wound between the ponderosa pines and aspen, the New Yorkers found themselves in front of the beautiful log home where they would live. The five humans and their dog emerged from the car. Nick and his family stood still for several minutes, taking in their surroundings with every one of their senses. Their skin reveled in the warmth of the sunshine. They heard birds chattering in the trees, pine needles rustling in the breeze, and crashing in the Big Thompson River as ice-cold water tumbled over the rocks behind the cabin. Deep breaths of the thin, aromatic mountain air refreshed and exhilarated them.

The cabin was nothing like their brownstone on the west side of Central Park. The exterior was built of whole logs. From there, any reference to a cabin was an extreme understatement. The house rested on a foundation covered with river rocks that had been sanded smooth by the force of the snowmelt in the spring. Each stone was just big enough to fit a man's grasp. A covered porch extended across the front and was home to handcrafted log furniture. While the family gawked, their Standard Poodle, Belle, completed three laps around the perimeter of the enormous house, searching for unsuspecting squirrels to chase.

Nick was the first to find his tongue. "Wow, Dad, this cabin is awesome!"

Nick's mother, Jeannie, chimed in, "Yes, Tom, how did you find such a fabulous place?"

"Talent, my dear, talent," Tom added. "Well, let's not just stand here. What do you say we go into our summer home?"

Once inside, the family stopped again. They stood with their eyes wide and mouths open, gazing around the interior. A large stone fireplace extended two stories to the beamed ceiling above. The rest of the house was equally extraordinary. The open floor plan included a huge gourmet kitchen, dining area, and living room. All four bedrooms were upstairs. Each door opened onto a balcony overlooking the main floor. To a boy such as Nick, raised in a tall, narrow brownstone, houses like this were beyond anything he ever imagined.

However, Nick soon found that he spent very few daylight hours in the beautiful house. Nearby, a local stable offered trail rides into the National Park. For a fee, any city slicker could step up on the mounting block, swing their leg over the western saddle cinched to a well-seasoned quarter horse or appaloosa, grip the horn, and ride to places most people couldn't find on foot. Rides lasted from one hour to overnight, depending upon what the pocketbook and the seat bones were able to endure.

Nick and his family were not the normal summer people that the stable owners, Larry and Carol Crisp, were accustomed to dealing with. Encouraged by their mother, Nick and his younger sisters, Lynn and Nancy, took riding lessons once a week all during the school year at the only riding stable left in Manhattan: The Claremont. This stable, on the west side of Central Park, opened in 1892 as a livery stable and, for nearly a century, had been a functioning riding academy for the luckiest New Yorkers. On the second floor of a four-story, historic building, surrounded now by high-rise apartments, the Claremont offered English riding lessons, including jumping and dressage. Once accomplished enough, riders were allowed to go on horseback the two blocks to Central Park for a hack on the trails there.

As a young child, Nick took to riding immediately. He seemed to understand just how to use his body to communicate with a horse. He had natural balance and rhythm and, with instruction, learned to use his weight and leg position to direct the horse forward and use his hands lightly to control the power beneath him.

Larry and Carol's horses were not the spirited, sensitive power machines that Nick had progressed to in his riding. And the heavy western saddle made it hard to feel the horse beneath him the way he was accustomed to with his English saddle. But a horse is still a horse and, to a horse lover, that is enough.

The first summer, Nick spent nearly every day at the Crisp's and soon was grooming and tacking-up the horses. Before long, he was assisting the trail guides on the group rides.

Nick's talent was not lost on the stable owners. He was soon allowed to ride the greenest horses and help train them to become trail savvy. "Green" is a horseman's term for a young or untrained horse. Becoming a trail horse in Rocky Mountain National Park is not that different from being a stable horse in Manhattan and walking through the busy streets to arrive in Central Park. A horse has to learn to ignore the external stimuli and trust and obey its rider, whether faced with a honking taxi or a bellowing elk. One horse and rider team must negotiate curbs, manhole covers, and icy streets, while the other must maneuver up rocky inclines, over fallen trees and across cold, fast-flowing streams. Nick, with the innocence of youth, figured he could handle anything Rocky Mountain National Park had to offer since he had survived the concrete wilderness of New York City.

The second summer did not arrive quickly enough for the New York family. As they flew across the country, Nick pressed his nose against the acrylic window of the jet, searching the ground below for the first sign of the snow-covered Rockies.

"There it is. There's Denver. We're almost there!" he said with excitement as he elbowed his sister. Lynn leaned forward to catch a glimpse of the mountains for herself just as the pilot came over the intercom to announce that they were beginning their descent, a fact that their popping ears and the bouncing plane soon confirmed.

Nick rubbed his hands together with anticipation during the drive up to their Estes Park cabin. He helped unload the car quickly, waved a "See ya later" to his family, and ran to the Crisp's stable.

Carol saw him coming down the dusty road and stepped out of the office. Standing on the wooden planks that formed the porch, she waited for him to reach her. Without taking the time to express her joy at his return, she simply said, "I have a surprise for you. Follow me."

Carol never walked slowly, but today she moved more quickly than usual and Nick had to jog to keep up as she led the way around the barn to the round pen. What Nick saw in the pen made his heart skip a beat. There, trotting around the pen with his head held high, was the most beautiful horse Nick had ever seen. The animal was large, maybe seventeen hands at the withers. A "hand" is the equivalent of four inches. The horse was dark bay, nearly black, with large, soft, kind eyes. When he moved, he seemed to float. This was no school horse or trail horse!

"How do you like him?"

"He's awesome," was all Nick could say.

"His name is Jazz. He's a Hanoverian, a German breed, bred for that dressage that you like. He's retired now, but he's had quite a show career. He was a Grand Prix champion."

"What's he doing here?"

"His owner was a school friend of mine. She wanted him to spend his last years with me, away from the arena and the horse shows, just bein' a horse in the great outdoors. If you're up to doin' some training, I'd like to turn him over to you to teach him about trails. He needs too advanced a rider to be any good to me right now, but he has a heart o' gold and a good head on 'im. He just needs experience on our Rocky Mountain trails."

Nick immediately knew what a great opportunity this was. He climbed up on the paddock fence and leaned over the top rail. Carol stood beside him, resting one dusty boot on the bottom rail.

"Hey, Jazz, come over here, boy," said Nick.

Jazz picked up his head and pricked his ears forward. Calmly, he walked over to where Nick was leaning toward him. He stopped right in front of the young boy. The beautiful gelding immediately dropped his head and began chewing and licking, a sign of submission. Nick reached out one hand and rubbed the gelding's face between his eyes. His fingers tickled the two cowlicks that swirled in different directions right in the center of the horse's forehead.

"Ah, you noticed the double cowlicks. There's an old Indian legend that a horse with double cowlicks is one of the noble and great ones," said Carol as she, too, reached up to stroke the large head.

Carol left the paddock fence and disappeared into the tack room. She came back carrying a black dressage saddle. "Well, I can say one thing for these saddles; they're a lot lighter than our western ones," she said as she handed the saddle over to Nick.

After being tacked up, Jazz stood perfectly still while Nick placed his left foot in the shiny, silver stirrup, bounced up and swung his right leg over Jazz's back. He gently sat down in the saddle. With a slight press of his calves against Jazz's sides, the gelding moved forward in a strong, brisk walk. Even at twenty years old, this highly trained horse moved with power and grace. With a gentle hold on the reins, Nick allowed his hands to follow the natural movement of Jazz's head and neck.

Carol leaned on the round pen's fence, watching the whole process with respect and admiration for this young East Coast horseman. Horse people know a true horseman no matter where they hail from or what type of saddle they use. And Carol recognized the talent Nick had in him.

"He has the horse gene, Tom," she said to Nick's father later that afternoon as the two of them watched him work with Jazz in the round pen. Tom, who obviously *did not* have the horse gene, glanced sideways at this cowgirl incredulously.

After a few days of working in the round pen, Nick took Jazz on his first short trail ride. Carol came with him on her favorite lead horse, Kit, as they introduced Jazz to the trail. Carol's horse was a large black-and-white appaloosa, the alpha mare of the herd. As they started out of the stable yard, Kit flattened her ears back against her head, bared her teeth, and tossed her head toward Jazz. The new horse immediately threw up his head and stopped dead in his tracks. From then on, he obediently stayed a few yards back from the mare's steel-clad back hooves while Kit constantly swished her stubby appaloosa tail to make sure this new horse in the herd wasn't within striking distance.

The powerful bond that can form between horse and human formed quickly between Nick and Jazz. Jazz needed a new leader and Nick needed a best friend. Nick began taking him alone on the familiar trails used by the trail guides. Jazz learned to cross a Rocky Mountain stream, picking his way over the slippery rocks. He learned to bend his body around a tree without causing his rider's knees to bang into the trunk. He learned to accept that deer and elk sometimes surprised him by bounding or strolling across the trail. He learned that the big horn sheep can scale a rock face high above him, and he learned to ignore the chatter of squirrels or the shrill screech of a falcon.

Each morning, Nick arrived just as the sun was turning the mountains a bright pink. He always found Jazz staring over the top rail of his paddock, his breakfast of grain and hay already finished. On this particular morning, as soon as Nick was visible around the side of the barn, Jazz shook his beautiful dark bay head up and down and let out a soft, low nicker. Nick went to him and Jazz pressed his muzzle against Nick's face and blew out a soft, warm stream of air from his nostrils. Nick cupped his hands around the velvet skin and held Jazz's head in his hands for a minute, looking into his large, dark eyes.

Nick gave Jazz a pat on the neck and reached for the halter that hung on the gate. "Let's go to the mountains, buddy," he said.

One of Nick's favorite trails in the southeast section of the national park was in an area called Wild Basin. He loved to ride along the Blue Bird Lake Trail because the path wound past numerous waterfalls and made its way above the timberline to Ouzel and Blue Bird Lakes. Beautiful log bridges had been built by the forest service, spanning from cliff to cliff in front of the waterfalls. They were a test for any experienced trail horse, but Jazz had learned to trust Nick. So, as they approached the first bridge in front of Calypso Falls, Jazz hesitated for only a moment before he responded to the gentle squeeze of Nick's calves and stepped onto the bridge that spanned across the front of the long and loud waterfall.

Nick and Jazz climbed up the trail until they passed all of the waterfalls and left most of the hikers behind on this especially hot summer day. The temperatures in Denver were climbing to over one hundred degrees and, even in the high altitude of the park, they were nearing ninety. Because of the threat of afternoon thunderstorms, Nick had left the stable with Jazz earlier than usual. They were now all alone on the stretch of trail that climbed above the tree line toward the lakes and mountain meadows.

Nick rode along, enjoying the beauty of the scenery and feeling the power of the horse beneath him. Jazz was moving up the trail in a marching walk in an attempt to keep the deer flies from biting his legs and belly. He frequently shook his head to use his forelock as a fly swatter for his face. Nick let his perfect English riding posture lapse as his torso moved in rhythm with the horse. He felt secure on Jazz now and didn't feel like he had to be on the alert every minute. Riders call this being "loose in the saddle." He was in this position when they passed by a large rocky outcropping. Suddenly, Jazz's head came up with a snort. His ears pricked forward and he came to an abrupt halt.

"It's okay, boy," said Nick soothingly, though still lost in his own thoughts. "Everything's okay, just a shad..."

He didn't have a chance to finish his sentence before a loud, deep growl sounded in his ears. At the moment he heard the noise and before he had a chance to react, a large, golden mountain lion sprang from its perch in the rocks above them and crashed against Nick's body. The force of its pounce took both the boy and the lion several feet through the air before they landed to the side of the trail. Nick hit the ground hard with the mountain lion on top of him. A loud grunt escaped his lips as the air was pushed out of his lungs. His instincts took over as he brought his hands up and took a firm hold of either side of the lion's head in a desperate attempt to keep the mountain lion's sharp teeth from reaching his face. The lion's face was no more than six inches from his. He looked into the fierce brown eyes and he felt saliva drip on his nose and cheeks. The young teen was no match for the lion. Nick could feel the lion's front claws rip through the fabric of his shirt and tear at his shoulders. The lion shook his head in an attempt to free himself from Nick's hold.

As suddenly as it began, the attack on Nick was over. The boy lay on the ground, staring in disbelief as Jazz picked up the beast with his teeth at the center of the lion's spine. The horse's strong jaws clamped together like a vice as he raised the lion into the air. The lion let out a piercing growl as Jazz violently shook the helpless yellow body and threw him several yards away. The big cat struggled to stand up on his feet, but Jazz was on him again pounding the lion's ribs with his steel-rod-like front legs and sharp hooves. The lion's snarls grew in volume and intensity as he fought for a foothold. Once he found his feet, the large, yellow lion made no attempt to fight back against this black fury with its ears pinned back, teeth bared, and nostrils flaring. The badly injured cat scrambled down the hill and stumbled over a steep ridge. Jazz reared in place and pawed the air as he watched the mountain lion retreat, letting out a loud, threatening neigh.

As soon as the threat was gone, Jazz lowered his front legs to the ground and walked over to Nick. The horse's body was shaking and covered with sweat as he lowered his head and blew warm air into Nick's face. Nick struggled to his feet, threw his arms around the horse's neck and buried his face in his mane.

"Jazz….Jazz," he gasped. "You saved my life. You saved my life."

— chapter 2 —

Transitions

ountain lion attacks are rare in Rocky Mountain National Park. As a result, word spread quickly among the park rangers and tourists. New signs went up at trailheads, warning people of the potential danger and what to do if they should see a lion. The lion that had attacked Nick was hunted down. Its body was found not far from the site of the attack.

Nick's injuries were minor. He had eight fairly deep scratches from the lion's claws that required antibiotic cream but no stitches. Other than that, sore muscles from the fall to the ground were all he could complain about.

Nick and Jazz became local celebrities around Estes Park. News reporters from all of the Denver stations wanted interviews and video of the boy and his "lion-eating horse." Even friends from New York called to check up on him when the story was aired back East. Nick knew that Jazz deserved all the credit and made sure that the media outlets understood as much. As for Nick, the new nemesis in all of his nightmares now changed from spiders to mountain lions, a much larger though less-insidious foe.

Nick's parents, who had never thought that Nick would be in any danger on his daily rides in the mountains, suddenly became irritatingly protective. "Do you need to go alone on the trail today? Why don't you stay with the group? Better yet, why not stay here with us?" his mother asked.

Nick committed to stay with the group as long as the lion's claw marks remained visible on his back. This compromise bought off his mother and let Nick keep his manly pride intact as the red lines remained a badge of fame and honor for the rest of the season.

As the end of the summer approached, the people of the charming town of Estes Park decided to host an art fair to encourage more tourism. The first night of the fair, Nick's family put on their sweaters to keep warm in the cool evening air and biked to the town green. Colorful booths were set up in a serpentine pattern throughout the little park and hundreds of people were milling around admiring, and frequently purchasing, the lovely works displayed by the artists and craftsmen.

Nick had been raised in the art museums of New York City and had a great appreciation for the talent possessed by others. His dad had always expressed a desire to paint, though his job had never given him the free time to develop that interest. "Someday," he always said.

Nick walked along with his family for a while, stopping at each booth to admire the works. There were displays of paintings, pottery, stained glass art, and bead work. Just about every type of medium and craft was represented. Some of the artists were local; others had come from places far and wide.

As his parents discussed the purchase of a watercolor painting of Long's Peak, something out of the corner of his eye caught Nick's attention. He turned his head and noticed an old man beckoning with an arthritic finger from the next booth. The man was seated on an old metal chair that had once been a bright yellow. His wavy hair was silver. The gray whiskers on his face indicated that it had been many days since they had met a razor. His blue eyes nearly disappeared when the old man smiled, which he was doing now. In one wrinkled and gnarled hand he held a pocket-sized knife, in the other a piece of wood. Nick looked at the table beside the man where his wares were displayed. He appeared to have one specialty: wooden unicorns.

Nick tapped his mom on the shoulder, "Mom, I'm going over to look at that booth." His mom gave a cursory glance toward the booth to which Nick pointed, nodded her head, and went back to discussing where they could hang the painting in their New York brownstone.

Nick stepped over to the booth. The man was looking down as he resumed carving but he was still smiling. Nick stood in front of the table, looking over the dozens of unicorns on display. "Did you carve all of these?" Nick asked.

"Sure did," responded the old man as he continued to work.

One of the unicorns caught Nick's eye. The figure had been carved in a dark wood and polished until it shone — a prancing unicorn, his neck arched, mane and tail flying. The unicorn reminded Nick of Jazz. He picked up the carving and turned it over and over slowly in his hands. The workmanship was beautiful. The man obviously knew horses for he had carved every detail of the body perfectly from the muscular shoulders and haunches to the delicate legs. The ears on the unicorn pointed forward, the nostrils flared, and the eyes seemed alive.

"You're the boy that survived the lion attack." This was said as a statement not as a question as the man continued looking down at his work.

"Yes, sir," Nick responded, accustomed to recognition from strangers by this time.

The man continued carving, sending little chips of wood to the littered ground between his feet. "That must be a remarkable horse you have there. I am sure that he loves you very much. I don't doubt that he will be a unicorn himself, someday."

Nick let out a soft chuckle.

The man stopped carving and lifted his head. His bright blue eyes bore into Nick. "What? Don't you know the legend of the unicorns?"

Nick shook his head, still holding the image of Jazz in his hands.

The old man set down his knife and the block of wood. He wiped his hands on his cream-colored tunic. He scratched his beard and smiled. "Well, my boy, legend has it that the most noble and great horses are trained to become unicorns when they leave this Earth. Once their training is complete, they receive their horns. From then on, they become the guardian angels to the animals." Motioning toward the unicorn that Nick held in his hands he said, "Tell me, does that horse of yours have a double cowlick right in the middle of his forehead?" As he talked, he raised a crooked finger and touched his own forehead.

Nick swallowed hard and nodded.

"Just as I suspected. Mark my words: that horse of yours will be a unicorn someday."

Nick's mother came up behind him and placed a hand on his shoulder. "What have you found there?"

Nick held opened his hands. "This carving looks like Jazz as a unicorn," he said, keeping his eyes on the old man who had returned to his work, a smile still on his face. The man lifted his sparkling blues eyes for a moment and winked at Nick.

High in the branches of a thick pine tree that sheltered the old man, four tiny fairies, each a different color, watched the festivities. The humans below were unaware of their presence.

The school year seemed especially long to Nick as he dreamt of returning to Colorado and Jazz. The boy waited impatiently for the time to come that he could be reunited with his horse. For Christmas, Nick's parents surprised him with the wooden carving of the unicorn that Nick found at the Estes Park art fair. Nick was overjoyed and he placed the figurine on his desk where he could see it from every angle in his room. Each time he looked at the shiny wooden statue, he thought of Jazz and the legend of the unicorn.

When summer finally came, Nick hurried back to the Crisp's stable to see his horse. Jazz greeted him with a nicker and a nudge of his soft muzzle as though they had never been apart. The nine months' absence had done nothing to lessen the bond between them.

The rest of Nick's family was equally entranced with Colorado. They loved exploring all that Estes Park had to offer, from the delightful Saturday morning brunch at the historic Stanley Hotel to shopping in the charming stores along the river walk. Each day, late in the afternoon, a large herd of elk roamed into the town and made themselves comfortable grazing on the fresh green lawn of the town square. This was always a popular event with the tourists. The family hiked all through Rocky Mountain National Park and reveled in the magnificence and beauty of the mountains. Evenings, the New

Yorkers went fishing, roasted marshmallows over a campfire, or played games around the dining table in the cozy great room of their log house. A fire blazed in the enormous fireplace, taking the chill out of the night air in the mountains. Near the end of each summer, the family attended the art fair. Nick never saw the old man and his unicorns again.

The summer that Nick turned seventeen would be the last. Nick had grown over the school year and had left his gangly teenage look behind. He was now a tall, handsome young man. His hair was neatly trimmed around the ears and across the back of the neck. The top was left long enough to show off the brown curls. His hazel eyes were deep-set beneath a high forehead. His jaw was strong yet soft. When he walked into the stable yard that June day, he did so with a new air of quiet confidence. A beautiful, wide smile filled his face as Nick was greeted by Carol with a big hug. She immediately noticed the change from boy to man that had taken place since their last meeting. Smiling to herself yet not wanting to say anything for fear of embarrassing him, she simply said, "Your horse is waiting for you."

Grinning broadly, Nick set off at a jog to find Jazz. The long-awaited reunion was joyous. As soon as Jazz saw the young man he let out a deep nicker and ran to the gate of the paddock. Nick threw open the gate and wrapped his arms around the dark bay gelding's neck. Jazz tucked his head and nuzzled Nick's shoulder. Nick stepped back and examined his horse. The dark bay coat was now dotted with gray hairs and the muscles along the once-strong back were now soft and weak, allowing the spine to dip slightly. But the love that radiated from Jazz's eyes was as strong as ever.

The last week of the summer arrived all too quickly for Nick. Monday began as a typical day in Colorado. The bright, clear sky was a vibrant blue but there was a touch of crispness in the air, indicating that fall was on its way to the Rockies. Nick waved goodbye to his parents and younger sisters as the rest of the family drove off to spend the day visiting the Museum of Nature and Science in Denver. He turned on his heel and headed out to ride Jazz. Their ride in the mountains went well and Nick noticed with sadness the first gold leaves appearing on the aspens. This was the sign he always dreaded seeing. This was the indication that the end of their time at Estes Park was nearing again for another year. He hated leaving Jazz behind, even under the careful care provided by Carol.

All of these thoughts were running through his head as he rode Jazz back into the stable yard later that afternoon. He saw Larry and Carol standing side by side, looking at him. He immediately noticed the ashen pallor to their faces and the grim expressions they wore. They stood stoically in front of the office looking eerily like Grant Wood's often parodied painting "American Gothic," sans pitchfork.

Nick didn't remember the exact words they used. All he was able to register in his mind were the essentials: "head-on collision…all dead." He turned his horse around and dug in his heels. Jazz leapt forward.

How long he and Jazz cantered through the woods he didn't know. His breathing was being dictated by Jazz's breathing and his heart beat with Jazz's heart, as though the horse was keeping him alive. For a long time it seemed as though nothing else existed. Slowly, the horse's strength seeped into Nick and he started to become aware of his surroundings. He looked around and realized he was on a trail he had never seen before. This path was narrow and nearly overgrown in places. Along the south side rose a high granite cliff, the base of which was littered with boulders of various sizes that had fallen off the rock face. At times he heard the pounding of a waterfall as gusts of wind carried the sound to his ears.

Slowing to a much-needed walk, Jazz wound his way ever farther up the trail. Soon the trail was traversing the cliff, which rose high on one side and dropped steeply down to the river on the other. The trail followed along the ledge until it rounded a point. There, in front of them, was the largest waterfall Nick had seen in the Park, nothing compared to Niagara Falls in upstate New York, but large by Colorado standards. At the base of the falls, water bounced off piles of granite boulders and the spray formed a thick mist. Across the mist, as though it had been painted, was a bright and beautiful rainbow. A rainbow…God's promise…God. *Where was God today?* thought Nick.

For the first time, anger welled up inside of Nick and his heart was pierced with a pain so intense he began to sweat. Jazz, sensing this change in his partner, stepped into a trot so suddenly that Nick was nearly thrown out of his always-perfect position. They trotted up the trail, which began zigzagging toward the left side of the waterfall. Yet every time Nick, with clenched teeth, looked toward the waterfall, his eyes were drawn to the base and there, in the mist, was the rainbow.

They finally reached the top of the cliff and found themselves well above the tree line. Nick knew that Jazz was struggling with the high altitude. Tree line meant they were over eleven thousand feet above sea level and, even though he was now acclimated to higher altitudes, this was higher than he had ever been with Jazz. He consciously calmed himself so he could pass this calmness on to his horse. Jazz slowed to a walk, lowered his head and began taking large, deep breaths. This wonderful, loyal horse had given his all to his friend, but he was feeling the effects of his efforts and his age.

Nick began stroking Jazz's neck. "It's just you and me now, boy. I need you now more than ever. What am I going to do? I'm alone…alone except for you." With that, a loud groan arose from deep within him and Nick began to cry.

Jazz stopped, turned his head around to one side, and placed his muzzle on Nick's boot. Nick bent forward, wrapping an arm around either side of Jazz's neck and buried his face in the black mane. They stayed that way for a long time while Nick's body shook with sobs, and tears wet the horse's shoulder.

As he wept, clouds silently formed and rolled over them. The grieving pair was in too much pain to notice the change in the weather until the first bolt of lightning and the immediate clap of thunder brought them back to the world around them. Jazz's head jerked up, his ears pricked forward and, for the first time, he whirled. The storm landed right on top of them. Darkness surrounded them, broken only by the intermittent flashes of lightning and the deafening sound of the thunder as it bounced and echoed off the cliff. Jazz began cantering down the trail. The wind muffled the sound of the waterfall. The rain that followed soon after made the trail slippery and difficult to negotiate for the otherwise sure-footed horse. Nick continued to cling to Jazz's neck, not thinking how hard this was for his horse as Jazz tried to keep his balance going down the hill.

Nick was in this position when the wet, muddy trail along the edge of the cliff collapsed beneath the gelding's feet. All Nick knew as he desperately clutched at the reins was that they were falling toward the base of the waterfall. He didn't notice that the rainbow was still glowing brightly.

⟤ chapter 3 ⟤
Behind the Mist

The first feeling that Nick was aware of was softness. He was surrounded by softness, as though he was floating not on a cloud, but *in* a cloud. Slowly his senses sharpened and he realized that he was lying on his back on a feather-filled down mattress and that he was covered with a thick down comforter.

Every part of his body felt warm. The warmth was wonderful and he took great pleasure in the sensation. His mind started taking inventory of each part of his body to see if everything was still there. He became aware of the warmth around his shoulders and chest and abdomen. He became conscious of the position of his arms and hands and, lastly, his legs and feet. From the messages his brain was receiving, his body was intact. He knew this was good news, but he didn't remember why he should be concerned. For what seemed like a long time, he just let himself experience the soothing comfort and welcome feelings that surrounded him, as though he were being held snugly in his mother's embrace.

Eventually, Nick became aware of sounds outside of his cloud of comfort. He gradually realized that the sounds were voices speaking in a language that was unfamiliar to him. He listened for a long time and, as he did so, his mind began to translate for him. He realized that he could understand what they were saying, even though the words were new to him.

"How is the boy doing?"

"He still has not awakened, but all of his vital signs are good and his injuries are all healed."

"You have done a good job, Shema. Thank you for your conscientious care."

"Oh, Mastis, it was you who healed him. Yes, indeed, it was all you. I only followed your meticulous instructions. By the way, perhaps it is not my business to ask, no, not my business at all, but have you met with the Council yet?"

"No, they are waiting until the boy returns to good health. They plan to meet with us together."

"Well, I wish you luck."

"Thank you, Shema, but I am not worried. I know the Council will always make the decision that is best for all concerned. I will check on our patient later. Let me know if there are any changes."

The voices stopped and were replaced by the quiet humming of a lullaby that Nick had never heard before. The music swirled around his head as if beckoning him to follow. He let his mind obey and he felt his eyes open of their own accord.

At first his eyes could not focus on all the visual stimulation at once. What he saw before him looked like an impressionist painting, with the edges of the objects blurred together by the light bouncing off of them. Every color ever created by the division of light surrounded him, and the objects they represented seemed to change their shape with the rise and fall of the music. Nick blinked his eyes several times and the forms around him began to gather their colors together and hold their position.

The lullaby continued and the visual sensations began to make sense to Nick. All around him were trees and flowers of every size and color imaginable. Some flowers, like the roses and day lilies, were familiar, but others were unlike any Nick had ever seen before. Slowly, Nick turned his head to his left, toward the source of the humming. An involuntary gasp left his throat.

"Well, well, well, you're finally awake. Mastis will be so excited, so excited, indeed! We've been waiting for you to join us for such a long time."

Nick shook his head and squeezed his eyes shut, but when he opened them, the scene had not changed. Nestled on the flower-filled grass before him was a unicorn. Her body was a golden brown and her pearl-colored mane and tail were long and flowing. The thick forelock that nearly reached her muzzle parted in the center. The shiny, coarse hair cascaded down her face, parted by the long spiraling horn that grew straight out between her large brown eyes.

"Oh, my poor boy, my poor, poor boy. This must be quite a shock to you, considering where you have come from." She shook her head as she looked at him with her soft brown eyes. "Yes, quite a shock, indeed. You have never been in the presence of a unicorn before. None of the horses you have known have earned their horns yet."

Nick finally gave voice to his first thought: "Where am I?" He heard himself speak though he didn't recognize the melodic tone of his voice, which almost sounded like a lullaby as well. He reached up and rubbed his ears.

"You are in the land behind the mist. We call this kingdom 'Celestia.' Mastis found you and your horse and brought you here to be healed. We knew we could heal you, but, oh my, we didn't think it would take so long. My, my, a very long time."

Nick struggled to push himself up with his arms, but found he was too weak to do so alone.

"Slowly, my boy, slowly. I will help you. Soon you will be strong, but right now you are still recovering."

"What happened to me?" Nick asked as the unicorn floated over and eased him up into a sitting position, using her front hooves like hands.

"You and your horse fell down the cliff into the mist at the base of the waterfall. Mastis was there to rescue your horse, but your horse absolutely refused to come through the mist without you. That is a remarkable horse you have there. He loves you deeply, yes, very deeply. I would guess the time will soon come when he is able to earn his horn. But, oh my, I always seem to get ahead of myself. Please forgive me. This must be confusing for you, very confusing indeed."

"Jazz? Where is Jazz?"

"He is here. He is all healed and spends most of his days looking after you. I have no doubt he will be back soon."

Suddenly visions of lightning and rain filled Nick's head, followed by the overwhelming sensation of falling. Nick began to shake and perspiration broke out on his forehead. He fell back onto the soft bed as he pressed his hands against his eyes in a futile attempt to erase the pictures in his mind.

"Oh dear, dear, dear, I have upset you. I have said too much; you are still too weak. Do not worry. I am here to take care of you. Mastis has given me that assignment, and I never shirk my duty, never ever shirk my duty."

"My family…where is my family?"

A look of sadness filled the liquid brown eyes of the unicorn nurse. "We sent the fairies to find out about you. They watched many humans search for you and your horse for countless, long days. People on horseback, others on foot, but none of them were your family. We later found out that your family…your mother, father, and two sisters… were killed the morning before your accident. They were killed in one of these 'chariots of fire' as we call them…those horrible things, those horrible, horrible things."

All of his memories came flooding back to him. Nick sat up. As though he were in a canyon facing the coming of a flash flood, Nick had the strong urge to run, to hide from the visions in his brain. He found himself gasping for breath as his arms and legs began shaking with tension. The tears came again and he buried his head in Shema's golden mane as he had countless days earlier with Jazz.

A velvet-soft muzzle blew warm air along his cheek and rubbed up and down from Nick's eyebrow to his ear and down to his chin. He continued to cry and his body shook. The gentle stroking of his face also continued.

After a long time, Nick drew large gulps of air into his lungs and he reached up to touch the muzzle that was caressing him. He turned his head and looked into Jazz's knowing eyes. Tears had wet the black hair from Jazz's eyes to his cheeks. Nick left the security of Shema's embrace and reached up to hug his old friend.

"Jazz…Jazz…Jazz."

"I am here with you. You are not alone."

Nick reared back and stared at Jazz. "You're talking to me? How did you do that?"

"Oh, I always talked to you. I am so happy that now you have the power to hear me."

"Yes," Shema added, "You have been healed, Master Nicholas, but you have also been changed."

"What do you mean, 'changed'?"

Jazz nuzzled him again, "There is much we have to tell you but we will save that for later. Besides, I'm sure Mastis wants to tell you himself. He was our savior," Jazz responded with reverence in his voice.

Later that day, Mastis returned to the beautiful grove of trees and flowers that had served as hospital and healing room. Mastis was a large, dappled-gray unicorn. His mane was black, and his tail was also black on the top half but the bottom was silver. All four legs were white nearly to the front knees and back hocks. His eyes were dark and sparkling. Centered on his forehead between those stunning eyes was a long, silver horn extending nearly two feet out from the base of his forehead. The horn glittered as though covered with tiny diamonds. As Mastis turned his head, light reflected off his horn and formed little rainbows in the air.

Nick watched the magnificent creature walk up to him as though he was moving to the music that floated through the air in Celestia. He moved so lightly that the grass and flowers did not even bend under his weight. Even though he was large, Nick felt only peace at his approach. He knew instinctively that there was nothing to fear from this glorious being.

As he reached Nick's bedside, his companions bowed low to the ground by extending their right forelegs forward, bending their left legs until their knees touched the ground. They lowered their heads until their muzzles also touched the ground. Nick sat, frozen, wondering how one greeted one's savior.

Clearly reading his thoughts, Mastis laughed and the tiny rainbows surrounding his horn burst outward in all directions. "Oh, Nicholas, you need not worry. Seeing you sitting up and looking so well is greeting enough for me. Greetings to you, too, Shema and Jazz. What a wonderful day it is to have Nicholas back with us, is it not?"

Nick marveled at Mastis's beautiful voice. His words sounded as though he were singing in a lovely tenor voice that would bring envy into the heart of any Broadway star.

"I have you to thank for saving Jazz and me, don't I?"

"I have no need of thanks from you. I have my reward just having you here with us. No doubt all of this seems strange to you and you must have many questions, both in your mind and in your heart. But do not expend any of your energy worrying. All of your questions will be answered in due time. Now you must simply rest and continue to gain your strength. Tomorrow will be soon enough to begin your instruction... after we have met with the Council."

"The Council?"

"Yes. We must meet with the Council of the Twelve Ancients and Urijah, the Lord of Celestia. They are looking forward to meeting you!" With a wink and a smile Mastis turned and, with a single bound, disappeared into the trees.

Nick spent the rest of the evening eating the milk, honey, cheese, and fruit that the beautiful unicorns of all sizes and colors continued to bring to him. Each unicorn was not only gorgeous, but seemed to sparkle in the sunlight. Even more interesting to Nick was that, as the sun went down, they continued to radiate light, like a Rembrandt portrait, with a light that seemed to come from within rather than reflected from an external source. As Nick pondered this, his eyes moved over to Jazz who lay nearby munching on some long sweet blades of grass. Nick blinked several times as he tried to make sense of what he was seeing. Jazz had changed. His dark bay coat no was no longer sprinkled with gray hairs. The muscles along his back were, once again, straight and strong. But, most remarkable of all, Jazz radiated the same light as the unicorns.

"Jazz! You are glowing, just like the unicorns. I have never seen anything so dazzling."

"My dear friend, you should look at yourself. You, too, are sending off the most beautiful rays of light."

Nick held up his left hand and took in a quick breath of air. With a feeling of fascination and wonder, he fanned out his fingers, wiggled them, clenched his fist then reopened his fingers. He held up his right hand as well and turned both hands so that his palms faced him. He placed his palms together and interlocked his fingers. As remarkable and impossible as all of this seemed, his hands had an aura around them just like he had seen with the unicorns and Jazz. He stretched out his hands and moved them over the down comforter that covered him. As he did so, the blanket lit up as though he were shining a light on the surface of the fabric. He grabbed the blanket and tossed it back to uncover his legs. He was amazed to see that his legs were also shining.

Nick threw himself back on the pillow. "What is going on around here? I really need to get some answers."

Jazz moved over to him and nuzzled him while blowing warm air through his nostrils. "I think tomorrow will be very enlightening for both of us."

⌐ chapter 4 ⌐

The Council

ick did not sleep much between marveling at his glowing hands and worrying about what the next day would bring. He spent a lot of time staring up at the stars as he thought about the strange place in which he found himself. As he stared, he noticed that he couldn't find any of the constellations that he was so familiar with from his nights of stargazing in the Rocky Mountains. Nothing about this place was familiar…except for Jazz. How thankful he was for Jazz.

When Shema arrived with a basket of cheese, fruit, and rolls for Nick, and a bucket of carrots and apples for Jazz, Nick was already up and moving restlessly around the grove. "Good morning. Good morning, my boy! You look wonderful, simply wonderful. I am so happy to see you up and about."

"Thank you for the breakfast but I'm not sure I can eat a thing. My stomach is rolling around inside of me."

"Suit yourself," said Jazz, "but I'll have mine, thank you."

"Shema, when will we go see the Council?"

"As soon as Mastis comes to retrieve you," she said with a smile. She swished her tail, shook her long, thick mane and trotted over to Nick. She encircled him with her head and neck and said in her beautiful musical voice, "Do not worry, my boy. All will be well. All will be well. You will love Urijah and the Council."

Nick put one arm over Shema's neck and stroked her face with his other hand. "Will you be there with me?"

"No, but Mastis will be there and they have asked that Jazz come as well."

As soon as the flowers opened for the day and the dew dried off of the leaves, Mastis floated into the grove. His eyes sparkled even more than usual as he greeted them. "What a wonderful day this will be for you. Are you ready?"

"I think so."

"Climb on my back and Jazz can follow us."

Grabbing a hunk of Mastis's thick black mane, Nick swung his right leg up and over the unicorn's back. He settled down onto the wide strong back and let his legs stretch down on either side of the muscular animal. In a flash they were off, cantering through the trees. Nick intertwined the fingers of both hands into the long mane. He couldn't help but lean from side to side to avoid the trees that whizzed by. Mastis chuckled. "Don't worry, Nicholas, I won't let you get hurt."

"Sorry, worrying is just a habit of mine." Nick felt his cheeks flush. He was embarrassed that he had displayed doubt in Mastis' ability. To avoid becoming too nervous, Nick closed his eyes. He concentrated on the feeling of power beneath him. Mastis's back was supple and strong as he galloped along. The unicorn moved swiftly along in perfect rhythm. He was so balanced, even with a rider, that Nick hardly noticed when he changed leads to negotiate a turn. Jazz followed closely behind them, but struggled a bit to keep up.

After a while, Nick decided he could trust himself to open his eyes. They were just nearing the edge of the forest and entering a large meadow that stretched to the horizon. The light-green grasses were dotted with wildflowers of all colors. As Mastis started across the meadow, a large group of what appeared to be birds arose from the grasses and fluttered away together.

"Fairies. You will meet them later," said Mastis.

While they galloped farther across the meadow, large granite boulders were visible, scattered across the landscape. As they continued on, the number of rocks increased and became larger in size. Nick saw a jagged cliff ahead of them. When they drew closer to the cliff, Nick could tell that what appeared to make the cliff look jagged were actually beautifully sculpted turrets. Most of them were large spires that looked like the unicorn horns. Each had been carved from multiple types of stone in different colors. They reminded Nick of the onion-shaped domes on St. Basil's Cathedral in Moscow that he had seen in pictures, though these were taller and thinner. Each combined two complementary colors: red and green, orange and blue, yellow and violet. Just as in a Van Gogh painting, the juxtaposition of the opposing colors caused each color to become more vibrant.

In the center of the base of the carved cliff was a large opening. Gold doors covered the cavity and a frame of jewels surrounded the doors. As they neared, the doors opened of their own accord and the party of three, dwarfed by the size of the entrance, slowed to a walk and passed through the entrance in the cliff.

The room inside was enclosed in stone but shone as bright as if it were outdoors. Marble columns of differing colors lined the two sides of the large entry hall. There were carvings on each column filled with depictions of unicorns. The floor was a beautiful mosaic made of shiny glass tiles. But the most glorious thing of all was overhead. The ceiling was thirty feet above the floor and formed a dome over the center of the room. Carvings of all different types of animals literally danced around the top of the walls. As Nick watched, one of the animals leaped out of line, crossed beneath the dome, and placed himself in a new spot in the line of stone animals. A few moments later, another animal did the same thing. None of the animals seemed to mind this periodic mixing of the order.

The dome was also something to behold. As Nick and Jazz watched, the color of the dome changed from yellow to orange, red to purple. Each time the surface changed colors, the dome sent out a field of sparkling stars that fell to the floor and sizzled as they landed on the glass tiles. Nick slid off Mastis' back and stood next to Jazz, frozen in place. The two watched with wonder and amazement. Mastis, enjoying seeing the astonishment in their eyes, smiled at his charges.

Beautiful music filled the room. This was apparently the source of the music that filled all of Celestia. The parade of stone animals along the ceiling seemed to be prancing in rhythm with the lovely melody.

Below this spectacle, unicorns moved in and out of the room, not seeming to be distracted by the magical animal sculptures above them nor the falling stars around them as they hurried about their business. They *were* distracted, however, by the young human visitor. Each unicorn turned to stare at Nick, though none slowed their pace or changed their direction of travel. Two large chestnut-colored unicorns with the same sparkling eyes approached the little group.

"Mastis and friends, welcome. The Council is expecting you."

With that, the two centurions turned and led the way through the entry hall toward the back of the room. Ahead of them were two more doors like the ones through which they had entered. These also opened ostensibly of their own accord. Nick gripped Jazz's mane tightly and looked over at Mastis.

Jazz seemed filled with excitement as he pranced lightly beside him, lifting his knees and hocks high and performing a movement called "piaffe" in dressage. Following Mastis' lead, they slowly stepped forward.

Once they were in the room, the doors closed behind them. Mastis halted and Nick and Jazz stopped beside him. Ahead of them were thirteen magnificent unicorns standing in a semicircle. Each was a different color and shone as beautifully as a gemstone, sending little patches of light all around the room like a crystal does when the sun strikes the different angles. However, there was no sun in this room. The light came from within each unicorn. In the center of the semicircle was the largest of all the unicorns. He was pure white with long hair, called feathers, covering each hoof. He had the characteristic long, thick mane and tail that all the unicorns possessed. These were also a radiant white. The only coloring on him was his pink muzzle, his large, gentle, blue eyes and the iridescent colors moving around on his horn. A wide, welcoming smile graced his face.

Mastis bowed low, his horn touching the mosaic floor. Nick and Jazz watched and followed his lead.

"Please arise, my friends. Welcome to the land behind the mist, dear Jazz and Nicholas. I am Urijah, the Lord of Celestia, the home of the unicorns who guide and serve the kingdom of the animals. You, Nicholas, have been the topic of much discussion among the Council." Urijah paused and turned his head from side to side, smiling at his Council. He turned back to Nick. "I am sure, Nicholas, that you have been surprised by many things since your arrival, not the least of which is your new ability to communicate with us. Perhaps you have also noticed that you are the only human in our kingdom."

Nick turned and stared wide-eyed at Mastis. Knowing the thoughts in Nick's head before he could even speak them,

Mastis answered for Nick, "Nicholas has not had much time to explore the kingdom. He wasn't aware that he is the only human with us."

"Ah, I see. Well, perhaps now you can understand why we have had so much to discuss concerning you. You see, my dear Nicholas, this is the highest kingdom to which animals may go after their Earth life. I, as a unicorn, am the Lord of this kingdom, which we call Celestia. I, and the Council of the Twelve Ancients, govern all of the animals here. The unicorns are the greatest of the Animal Kingdom. They were horses in their Earth life, but became unicorns because of the great love within their hearts. Jazz was one of those noble and great horses that learned to love so completely in life that he was chosen to come to Celestia and progress toward becoming a unicorn. It is because of his great love that you are here. You see, Nicholas, Jazz refused to come without you when Mastis was sent to escort him to our kingdom. When you were found in the mist at the base of the cliff, you were clinging to Jazz's neck. Both of you were fatally injured. Mastis, without consulting the Council first, I might add," Urijah interjected, not unkindly, "chose to bring you here with Jazz."

"Such has been done before, Urijah," Mastis interrupted.

Urijah paused, and looked a bit sternly at Mastis. The rest of the Council turned and looked at him as well, but it was difficult for Nick to read their expressions. He did notice that none of them were smiling and several of the Council averted their eyes to look over at the unicorn that stood stoically to Urijah's right. Nick glanced over at Jazz and the beautiful dark horse returned his glance with a questioning look in his eyes.

"Yes," Urijah answered slowly and all the unicorns looked back toward Nick and Jazz. "It has been done before and that is the source of our concern. However, let me continue with my thoughts for Nicholas' benefit." He turned back to Nick and said, "Nicholas, Mastis and his helper Shema have spent much time and much power healing you and giving you the new life you have now. You have now become immortal. You have great powers, most of which you are not yet aware you even possess. It will be up to you to learn all you can about your new abilities. But, of greatest importance, you must understand that it will be up to you to decide if you will use your powers to bring light into the kingdom or to bring darkness. If you choose the former, you may stay with us. If you choose the latter, you will be cast out into the darkness." Urijah paused as if to let Nick absorb what he had just been told. With a smile on his face he said, "Jazz's great love for you makes us feel confident that you will make the right choices."

Jazz nuzzled Nick's cheek and Nick felt as if he were, once again, wrapped with the softness of his down bed. All of the Council looked at him, and their light seemed to reach toward him as each nodded their agreement with the confidence that Urijah had placed in Nick.

"Thank you, my Lord. I will do my best to live up to your expectations," responded Nick as he bowed toward Urijah and the Council.

The unicorn to Urijah's right cleared his throat before he spoke. "Dear Nicholas, I am Helam." Nick looked up and into the warm brown eyes of the unicorn that now addressed him. Helam continued: "I supervise the instruction of our foals, as we call our unicorns who have not yet earned their horns. You and Jazz have much to learn. I have selected Mastis to be your instructor as he was your savior and has already learned to love you deeply."

Mastis turned and smiled at Nick and Jazz. This, obviously, pleased the large gray unicorn. "Thank you, Helam. I shall be honored to be their instructor. I have been planning for several days where to begin and I feel I have an excellent course of study prepared for them."

"Excellent, Mastis. I know that we can count on you to do a thorough job. Know that we, as a Council, are here to be of assistance to you whenever we are needed. Now, I believe the time has come to begin Nicholas and Jazz's education," concluded Helam.

"Nicholas and Jazz, we welcome you to Celestia and will be watching with much interest as you progress," said Urijah with a smile. His body sparkled and light radiated from him in all directions.

Nick, Jazz, and Mastis realized that they were being dismissed. They bowed as one and turned around. The immense doors opened and they walked back into the great hall and through the falling stars. When the Council room's doors closed, Nick stopped and turned toward Mastis.

"I know your thoughts," the great unicorn smiled, returning his gaze. "Urijah said that you are the only human in our kingdom, but you are not the first."

"Exactly. Tell me what he meant."

"Yes," Jazz chimed in, "we are very interested in that comment."

"Several seasons ago, we do not measure time the way you did in your earthly life, a young girl was brought to Celestia. She, too, had been beloved by a horse that had earned the privilege of becoming a unicorn. But, let me go back a bit further. You see, Nicholas, while learning the power of love may qualify a horse to come to the highest kingdom of immortals and progress to become a unicorn, our freedom to choose is never taken away from us. At any time, we can choose to use our power for good or for evil. We have the commission to serve the animals. It is not our commission to interfere with humans even though we have the power to do so. Some of our unicorns have not made wise choices and have wanted to usurp the role of humans as stewards over the Earth. They joined together behind a leader named Hasbadana and rebelled against the Council. As a result of their pride and disobedience, their light was taken away from them and they were cast out of Celestia and into the Dark Kingdom. They have been enemies of the light ever since. But, I digress. Let me return to the account of the other human. When the young girl was brought here, Hasbadana was able to turn her from the light." Mastis looked down and some of his light seemed to withdraw into him. "She now serves him."

A long silence followed as Nick and Jazz thought about what they had just heard. The weight of the responsibility that Nick had been given was just making itself felt. Above them, the dancing stone animals stopped in their circle and looked down at them.

"Mastis, do not worry. We will not let you down. We will use the light for good. You can depend upon us," Jazz assured him.

"I know you say that from your heart for I know that your heart is pure. However, choosing the light is not always easy. Let us hope your path will not be strewn with too many thorns."

～ chapter 5 ～
Training Begins

hen Nick, Jazz, and Mastis returned to the grove, they were greeted by a dozen or more unicorns all carrying baskets of food and ready for a celebration. Shema led the way. As she floated up to the trio, she set down her basket of fruits in front of Nick and wrapped her head and neck around him.

"Welcome to Celestia. Welcome, welcome to Celestia. We are having a celebration now that you and Jazz are officially part of our kingdom." She backed away from Nick and approached Jazz. She gave him the customary unicorn greeting, bowing to him until her horn touched the ground. Next, she placed her muzzle up to his and blew out a soft breath of warm air.

Jazz returned the greeting in the same way and said, "Thank you, Shema, we have much gratitude in our hearts for you and we will do our best to live up to the trust you have placed in us."

One by one, each of the unicorns that had gathered for the celebration presented their basket of food to Nick and Jazz. After greeting Jazz in unicorn fashion, they welcomed Nick with kind words of greeting. Nick's lack of appetite from the nervousness he felt in the morning was now replaced with a ravenous hunger as he started trying all the fruits, vegetables, rolls and cheese that had been placed before him. Jazz, too, helped himself to the bounteous and varied feast. Mastis, however, stepped back and watched the merriment as the unicorns sang and danced.

Once Nick and Jazz were finished eating, several of the unicorns pulled them into the circle to join in their dance. One of the unicorns scooped Nick up by placing his head and horn between Nick's legs and tossed him into the air. Nick came down gently onto the unicorn's back. Nick laughed with glee as the unicorns pranced in circles and patterns like a western square dance. He rode along, bouncing slightly to the rhythm of the music that filled every inch of the clearing. Even the trees seemed to move with the music.

Mastis observed from the side for a bit but soon began pacing back and forth. When his patience was spent, he called a halt to the gaiety. "Nicholas and Jazz, we have much to do and I would like to begin immediately."

Addressing the unicorns that had stopped their merriment and were now standing still and silently facing him he said, "I want to thank all of you, my friends, for the joyful celebration you have prepared. However, I'm sure you will understand if I take our foals with me to begin their training."

Each of the unicorns said their goodbyes. Jazz and Nick expressed their thanks before they followed Mastis out of the familiar clearing and into the woods. They walked silently behind the large gray unicorn as he gracefully worked his way between the trees. After a short walk, Nick noticed rays of light radiating toward them. Mastis led his foals to the edge of a large clearing, which turned out to be the source of the light.

The opening in the woods glowed so brightly that, at first, both Nick and Jazz had to squeeze their eyes shut until their pupils could adjust to the brightness. Once his eyes were able to take in the light, Nick looked into the clearing. The meadow appeared to be a perfect circle divided in half by a small stream. All of the flowers that grew wild on Earth that Nick recognized were present in abundance, but those familiar flowers represented only a small percentage of the flowers that filled the meadow. As Nick watched, flowers appeared from the ground as a bud, grew to their full height, burst open, and, just as quickly, wilted. This cycle repeated itself over and over in less than a minute's time. Due to the volume of flowers, the meadow was always full of the movement of buds bursting open.

Nick's attention was next drawn to the statue of an animal on a tall column. He looked further and noticed another column, and another column, until his eye was drawn past column after column around the entire circle. The animals that stood atop these columns were like the ones that danced around the dome in Urijah's palace. As Nick looked closer, he noticed that these statues could also move, even though they appeared to be secured to their pedestals.

"What is this place?" Jazz asked, breaking the silence.

"This is our schooling arena. Here I will teach you about the powers you have and how to use them," Mastis replied as he stepped lightly into the flower-filled meadow. "You will notice the animals that surround the edges of the arena. They represent the highest virtues we can possess. The dog represents loyalty. The cat represents cleanliness. The pig represents intelligence. The ox represents work. The eagle represents honesty. The turtle represents patience. The cow represents kindness. The lion represents courage. The elephant represents dependability. The horse represents love."

As he named each animal, Nick and Jazz let their eyes move from one statue to the next.

"Each of these animals has developed that virtue to the highest degree. Therefore, they inspire us to develop each virtue ourselves. You see, we don't come to Celestia as perfect beings. We have all of eternity to work toward perfection. You noticed the same sculptures in the dome at Urijah's palace. They are always placed in a circle to represent that each virtue is of equal importance. Horses that have the ability and disposition to develop each of these virtues are selected to come to Celestia and become unicorns. Once they become unicorns, they have the assignment to help all of the animals in the Animal Kingdom who have reached their life of immortality reach their highest potential. They must also be of assistance to the mortal animals on Earth."

Mastis paused and looked deeply into their eyes before he continued.

"Let me point out that, in Celestia, we have accepted and trained horses from every background. We have, in the Legion of the Unicorn, six of the eight Hanoverian Creams that pulled King George III of England's twenty-four foot long golden carriage in Earth's eighteenth century. We have thoroughbreds who have won America's Kentucky Derby. Yet, at the same time, we have the small, stocky horses that carried shamans across Mongolia and swaybacked plow horses that worked for farmers in South America. Their station in life matters not to us. It is what is in their hearts that we evaluate. Each of the horses who have joined the Legion now spends his time fulfilling their assignments to serve the animals in both their mortal and immortal lives."

"Do you mean you go back to Earth?" asked Jazz.

"Oh, yes, all of the time."

"Then why didn't we ever see unicorns when we were… *alive*?" Nick paused, unsure of what word to use.

"Alive?" Mastis offered with a chuckle. "It seems strange to use that word when you are still so much alive, doesn't it?"

"Yes, I guess that's the problem." Nick blushed.

"We refer to our past life as our 'Earth life' and this as our 'immortal life.' That makes it easier to distinguish between them. Now, back to your question regarding why you didn't ever see unicorns before you came to Celestia. You see, Nicholas, we unicorns have the power to make our immortal bodies invisible."

As if to illustrate the point, Mastis disappeared before their eyes. Nick caught his breath and Jazz let out a snort and whirled in a quarter circle. Mastis reappeared in the same spot with a big smile on his face. "Pretty incredible, is it not?"

"Do we have the power to do that?" asked Jazz while slowly turning on his haunches back toward Mastis.

"You will be given the power to do that and much more. We will start with simpler exercises before working up to that. Like in dressage, we will start with the training level and move up the levels to Grand Prix," replied Mastis with a smile.

Jazz shook his head up and down as if trying to put everything in place. Nick just stood there with his mouth open. Jazz reached over and nuzzled Nick's cheek, "Are you okay?"

Nick snapped his mouth shut. "I have a lot to become accustomed to," was all Nick could say in response. His brain was having trouble accepting all of this.

"We both do," responded Jazz as he wrapped his head and neck around the boy. Nick stroked Jazz's face and felt another rush of gratitude fill his body that he had his friend with whom he could experience all of this. Of course, he knew that had it not been for Jazz, he wouldn't even be here. Where he would be was a thought that was too big to wrap his mind around at this time, so he pushed the thought away.

"Well, let's begin our training," said Mastis as he trotted around in a circle to show his excitement. "Let's see...how to begin? I know! If, in your Earth life you were an architecture student studying Frank Lloyd Wright's work, you might attend a school called Taliesin West in Arizona. When you arrived at the school, you would be directed to a slab of concrete and told to create your own living quarters from the materials around you. I think that is what we shall do. Since humans are so accustomed to living in houses, the two of you shall create a house to live in here in Celestia. In order to create your house, you shall have to use the power that is within you to move and sculpt the raw materials around you."

To illustrate his point, Mastis pointed his horn toward a tree at the edge of the schooling arena. His eyes stared at the tree, and Nick and Jazz turned to follow his gaze. Suddenly, the tree started to move and bend. As the tree moved from its spot and came toward them, Jazz's head went up and he snorted as he backed several strides away.

Nick remained frozen in place. Once the tree was about twenty feet away from them, the trunk split down the middle and formed two conjoined arches about ten feet high by imbedding the branches deeply into the ground.

Slowly Nick turned to Mastis. "You mean we can make things move?"

"Oh, yes. All of creation, except humans of course, are at your command. But you must remember that love is the source of your power so all that you do must be done with love."

"But I don't have a horn yet," replied Jazz.

"Yes, the horn does make directing the power easier. But you will be able to control your power with careful concentration. Let's try. Begin by reaching deep within your heart to the center of your being. Feel the power that is there."

Nick closed his eyes and concentrated on feeling the love within him. He could feel the warmth in his heart as he thought of his family that he loved so deeply. He thought of friends. He thought of Jazz. He thought of the beauty of Earth. With each thought, he felt a power increase within him.

"Now, bring that power up to your brain and focus on a stone in the creek. Ask the stone to come slowly to you. Let's begin with you, Jazz."

Jazz stood straight on all four legs, his weight evenly distributed. His ears pointed straight ahead as he stared at a smooth, round, green rock close to the water's edge. Within a few minutes, the water's surface began to ripple and bubble. The rock rose straight up about twelve inches above the surface of the stream. It hovered there for a moment before slowly moving toward Jazz. The line the stone traveled was straight and it took only a few seconds to reach the beautiful horse. When it was a few feet away, Jazz blinked his eyes and lifted his head. The stone dropped to the ground.

"Well done, Jazz! That was marvelous. You are not only filled with great power but you are already able to begin controlling it," praised Mastis in his musical voice. "All right, Nicholas, it is now your turn."

Nick turned toward the brook and placed both feet firmly on the ground about a foot apart. He resolutely placed his hands on his hips, more for security than anything else, and picked a small red rock on the far side of the little stream. He stared at it as he gathered his power from deep within and brought it up to his brain. He focused his thoughts on the rock and instructed it to rise out of the water. At first nothing happened and he began to let go of his thoughts and concentration.

You have the power within you, Nicholas. Do not doubt yourself, he heard Mastis say from somewhere inside his brain.

This encouragement helped him to refocus his strength and thoughts. *Rock, come to me*, he said in his brain, *come to me*.

Suddenly, he could see the rock wiggle beneath the water. With a jerk, the little stone left its resting place under the water, rose into the air, and moved quickly toward Nick, who caught it in his hands.

"All right," exclaimed Nick as he tossed the rock in the air. Nick whooped and cheered as he and Jazz both began jumping around in circles, celebrating their victories.

Mastis watched with a pleased expression on his face as his two student foals congratulated and rejoiced with one another.

Finally, out of breath, but with big grins on their faces, Nick and Jazz stopped and turned toward Mastis.

"You now can see the power you have within you to influence the elements from which both Earth and our kingdom are created. As long as you use this power for good, it will be a great tool. But remember, the source of your power is love. If you lose the love, you will lose the power," said Mastis in a low voice, almost pleadingly. "Let us go back to your clearing to rest for the night. Tomorrow we will let you begin building your abode."

"Nicholas, you are tired, my friend. Let me carry you back," said Jazz with a nudge of his head against Nick's shoulder. The big, dark bay gelding bent his left leg and lowered it to the ground. Suddenly Nick realized how tired he was and he gratefully climbed up on Jazz's sturdy back, held onto his mane, and relaxed into the horse's rhythmic walk. After a short time, they were back in the clearing.

"It has been a most wonderful day, Nicholas and Jazz. Rest well. I will be with you again in the morning," said Mastis before he left them alone.

Nick slid off Jazz and onto his down bed. He curled up under the comforter and laid his head on the comfy pillow. Shema came into the clearing to see if she could bring him something to eat, but Nick was not even aware of her visit. He had fallen sound asleep as soon his head hit the pillow.

~ chapter 6 ~
Building a home

Nick was awakened by the bright light that reflected off Shema's and Mastis's glistening horns. He put his hand up to shade his eyes as they struggled to adjust to the multi-colored sparkles his nerve endings were sending to his brain.

"Good morning, good morning, my boy," Shema greeted Nick with her customary enthusiasm.

Nick stretched his arms and legs and smiled at his new friends. He loved hearing the beautiful, musical voices of the unicorns and watching their bodies sparkle in the sun. *What a great way to wake up,* he thought to himself.

"Good morning," he responded with a big smile. Nick stood up and put on the fresh white tunic that Shema held out to him. Since he had been in Celestia, his wardrobe had consisted solely of a white cotton tunic and tan pants. The tunic reached just below his hips and laced at his neck. The sleeves were full but gathered into a cuff at his wrist. Beneath this he wore slim, tan-colored pants that were a heavier fabric yet still quite comfortable. His feet, hands, and head were bare.

After freshening up in the basin of warm water, he joined Jazz and Mastis as they ate breakfast. Missing dinner the night before was a habit he did not want to develop as his newly immortal body was famished by breakfast time. He sat beside Jazz in the thick carpet of green grass and filled himself with the bread and fruit spread out in front of him.

"Well, Nicholas, today you and Jazz will begin to use your powers to create a home for the two of you."

"Do you have a house, Mastis?"

"All of Celestia is my domicile. I don't really feel the need for a structure to call home as you humans do, but I think this exercise will help you to develop and improve your skills as well as help you feel more at home in Celestia. I was extremely pleased with the abilities that you displayed yesterday."

"I didn't realize it would be so exhausting just to move a little rock."

"Yes, both you and Jazz slept well last night. However, as you become better at controlling your power, you will find that controlling the elements becomes easier. Now, tell me, where would you like to build your home?"

Nick looked over at Jazz. "Anywhere is fine with me, but I have grown quite fond of this little clearing," said Jazz in a quiet voice.

"I was thinking the same thing," replied Nick as he leaned back against Jazz's shoulder.

"Then here it shall be," stated Mastis enthusiastically. "I have brought you something that will help you begin." Mastis reached around with his neck and pulled a light-colored bag off his back. With the bag in his mouth, he shook his head quickly from side to side. As his forelock swished from one side of his horn to the other, four golden pinecones fell out of the bag and onto the ground in front of him.

"These pinecones will become your corner posts," he said with a smile. "Place them where you wish to locate the corners of your home."

Nick picked up the golden pinecones and placed the first one near his bed. Walking several strides in each direction, he and Jazz placed each pinecone on the ground, forming a rectangle. "Half of this will be for me and half will be for you," said Nick to Jazz. The dark bay shook his head up and down in agreement.

"Wonderful" said Mastis with enthusiasm. "Now the work begins. Within each pinecone is a gorgeous ponderosa pine just waiting to burst forth."

"But a pine tree takes years to grow," said Nick with skepticism.

"Ah, but only in Earth life. Here in Celestia, we need only provide the seeds with the power they need and they can quickly reach their potential. You must give the pinecones the power within you, instruct them as to how you want them to grow and they will obey. Remember, all power needs guidance and direction in order to be used for something great and useful. We call these directions 'commandments.' Obeying commandments is what helps everything reach its greatest potential and fulfill the measure of its creation." Mastis paused. "Do you remember your source of power?"

"Yes," replied Jazz and Nick as one. "Love."

"Yes, love is the source of all of your power. You may combine your love to increase your power. Humans on Earth often say that two heads are better than one. Well, I say that two hearts are better than one," said Mastis chuckling. Becoming serious once again he continued with his instruction. "Picture in your mind what you want the pinecone to become as part of your new home. The pinecone will obey you."

Nick and Jazz talked together for a few minutes as they designed the corner posts of their new home. "I think we should ask them to grow straight up for about ten feet, bend over toward each other and grow until their tips touch one another," suggested Nick.

"Yes, and we could ask them to intertwine their branches to form the roof," added Jazz.

"Do you think they could do that?" asked Nick of Mastis.

"They can do whatever you need them to do."

With that reassurance, Nick and Jazz stood side by side with Nick's right arm thrown over Jazz's neck. They put their heads close together as though the proximity to one another helped them be more united in their work. Nick took the roll of spokesman.

"Pinecones, we want you to grow from where you now lie, straight and strong for ten feet into the sky. We want you to turn your tips toward the center of the rectangle and grow toward each other until your tips touch and intertwine. Next, take your branches and form a tight roof over the top of the entire space…please."

With the commandments given, Nick and Jazz focused the power within them on each of the four pinecones at once. Nick felt the horse beside him grow tense as he focused his concentration. Nick turned his attention away from Jazz and, once again, directed his energy toward the pinecones.

Suddenly, each golden pinecone split open with a popping sound. A small light-green sprout appeared from the center. The little saplings began stretching themselves skyward, becoming thicker and straighter with each inch. By the time they reached five feet in height they had a circumference of at least a dozen inches and a reddish-brown bark already forming on their trunks. Once they reached ten feet in height, they were several times that thickness and the bark was brown and rough in appearance. As commanded, at this height the tops of the trees turned toward one another and grew at an angle until they joined in a point above the center of the rectangle.

From each trunk, branches began to sprout. They didn't grow out in all directions from the trunks, however. Rather, they grew in an orderly fashion along the planes of the roof angles. They interlaced themselves from the bottom of the roof to the top as their needles overlapped to form a living thatched roof. The smell of fresh pine filled the air and, in just a short time, a beautiful, living shelter stood before them. The four corner posts were straight and strong and the lovely thatched roof was tight and secure.

Nick nearly collapsed against Jazz with exhaustion and excitement. "Wow, Jazz, we did it," he exclaimed as he leaned against the strong dark shoulder of the horse. Jazz curved his neck around and smiled, his big brown eyes filled with both love and wonder. Mastis nodded in approval as he looked over the beautiful framework.

"Now you need to call up the rocks from below the ground to form your walls."

Nick and Jazz straightened up once again. "You do the sides and I will do the front and back," said Jazz.

Nick nodded and began focusing his power on the unseen rocks beneath the grass and flower-covered soil of the clearing. The earth began to shake gently beneath their feet. He stopped abruptly and looked over at Mastis with panic in his eyes.

"Don't worry, Nicholas. Remember, the elements will obey you and will not harm you if you command with love."

Shaking his head and letting out a long deep breath, Nick went back to work. The gentle shaking resumed. Beautiful rocks of many sizes and colors arose from the ground along the lines between the ponderosa pines. They fit themselves together, neatly, as they formed strong, thick walls. Openings were left for windows and doors. Clunking and scratching sounds rumbled through the clearing as the rocks positioned themselves to form walls on all four sides of their home. When the rocks reached the lowest beams of the roof, large rocks stopped erupting from the ground. Little rocks could be seen scurrying around to find a place to fit in at the last minute. This made Nick, Jazz, and Mastis laugh together.

As the rocks completed their task, the air was filled with what must have been a cheer but sounded more like a Mozart symphony because there were so many notes to the musical sound. Jazz and Nick took their focus off of their work and looked around them. All around the clearing stood more unicorns than Nick had yet seen in Celestia. Nick had been concentrating so hard on his work that he had not been aware of their arrival. The unicorns were cheering in their musical voices. Some were pawing the ground; others were rearing on their hind legs and pawing the air. A few were doing a piaffe, essentially trotting in place. Every one of them was celebrating Nick and Jazz's success.

Nick stepped back and looked at their new home. Before them, in the little clearing that had once been empty except for Nick's featherbed, there now stood a small but beautiful stone cottage. Rocks of all different colors glistened in the sunlight. A soft breeze caused the living thatched roof of pine needles to rustle gently. "Surely, this is the most beautiful and best-smelling house ever created," said Nick with a big smile while giving Jazz a pat on his neck.

"I have one improvement to make if you will allow me," Shema said with a smile.

She turned and pointed her horn toward the door. Soon a vine began growing up one side of the door, sending out tendrils that attached themselves to the rough rock walls. The creeping plant arched itself over the doorway and as it did so, roses of pink, red, yellow, and white bust into bloom with a backing of shiny, green leaves.

"Perfect, Shema, that is just what our home needed," exclaimed Nick and Jazz simultaneously while laughing with delight.

Nick abruptly stopped laughing. As he stood and looked at the beautiful pine trees that formed the roof of the lovely little cottage, the voice of his father entered his head with one of his favorite sayings: "If you look up and see pine trees and blue sky, life is good." His father said this each time they arrived in Estes Park to begin their summer soirée away from New York. He also said the same words each time they stopped during a hike to rest. Nick could feel his throat muscles constrict and he blinked his eyes to stop the stinging.

Mastis was immediately at his side. "Do not worry about your family. They are doing well," he said with his velvety muzzle rubbing Nick's cheek.

Nick took a deep breath and forced a smile. "I just miss them so…," Nick suddenly stopped. "Do you know my family? Do you know where they are?"

"Yes, my son. They are in the Human Kingdom. I have communicated with them. You do not need to worry. They know you are well and happy. But, now is the time to focus on your training." The beautiful unicorn changed the subject. "Go inside," Mastis said with a smile. "I have done some work of my own."

Jazz came up behind Nick and pushed him forward with his large head. Nick stumbled forward with a laugh and led the way into the cottage. Nick was stunned at what he encountered inside. The room was divided in half with a lovely stone wall that matched the exterior walls. In the middle of the dividing wall was a large archway, tall enough to enable Jazz to enter into his stall. But the most amazing thing was Nick's side of the cottage. In one corner was his fluffy down bed. Along the wall next to his bed his tunics and pants were hanging on wooden pegs. In the far corner was a pool of water that was constantly being filled from a stone pitcher that was attached to the wall. Even though it was always being filled with fresh water, the pool did not overflow. Nick rushed over to the pool and put his hand into the water. It was warm, the perfect temperature for a daily bath.

"Look up," said Jazz. Nick turned away from the pool and looked up toward the peak in the pine-thatched roof. There, hanging from the top point, was a Calder-like mobile of hanging crystals of all shapes that twisted and turned. As the mobile moved, it scattered rainbows all around both Nick's room and Jazz's stall.

Jazz's stall was also equipped with running water but this was in a much smaller pool and the water was cool. The entire floor was covered with deep straw and in one corner a bowl that held carrots and apples was attached to the wall. Even a Grand Prix Dressage horse wasn't treated to a stall this nice. Jazz helped himself to the treats and found that they were immediately replenished.

Nick turned and hurried out the doorway. He went up to Mastis and bowed his head. Mastis returned the bow. "Thank you, Mastis, we have a wonderful home."

Jazz came up and placed his muzzle next to the unicorn's muzzle and blew warm air into his nostrils. Then he, too, bowed in thanks.

After a filling dinner and words of praise from the other unicorns, Nick and Jazz retired to enjoy their first night in their new home. Nick disrobed and slipped into the pool for a long soak. As the warm water enveloped him, he felt his immortal body relax. He smiled as he watched his glowing body light the pool. For the first time, he noticed the intricate mosaic design that lined the pool. The sides were made from different colors of smooth glass tiles. *Mastis is amazing*, he thought to himself. He leaned his head back and closed his eyes, reveling in the warmth that surrounded him. "Jazz?"

"Yes, my boy?"

"Are you happy here?"

"This is more heavenly than I imagined Heaven could ever be. What about you?"

"I am so happy being with you, and the unicorns, and learning to use my powers for good, but..."

"But you miss your family."

"Yes. I hope they are learning as much as I am and that they are happy. Weren't you interested in the things that Mastis said about them?"

"I was indeed. But I am sure they are happy."

"You know, Jazz, it's my love for them and you that I draw upon to obtain my power."

"From my love for you and the other humans in my Earth life and my love for the mare that was my mother, I gain my power."

"Do you think I will ever see my family again? Do you think you will ever see your mother again?"

"Perhaps Mastis knows the answer to those questions."

A hush filled the cottage as Nick thought about his family. Quietly, he slipped out of his tub and put on a clean tunic. He walked silently over to his bed and sat down. After a moment, he lay back and looked up at the mobile that hung from the point of the roof. The beautiful work of art was constantly moving due to the careful balance of the attached pieces. As it twisted and turned, the crystals sent out little rainbows of color that danced all around the room. However, unlike the sun shining through a prism, this mobile sent out rainbows from its own internal light, even in the dark of night. Soon, the dancing rainbows had done their magic and Nick was fast asleep.

chapter 7
Fairies

Mastis continued to help Nick and Jazz refine their skills. They moved on from rocks and trees to other elements. Nick marveled at his ability to control the wind and rain. He learned to bring the moisture in the air together to form a cloud and command that cloud to rain on a tiny spot of ground. He called forth the water from the ground to form a beautiful fountain. The wind also obeyed his commands. At times he asked for a gentle breeze to move the wings of a butterfly. At other times he called for all the strength of a tornado to break apart a stone cliff.

After weeks of practice, it became increasingly easy to focus upon the power within him and thereby control the elements. Jazz, too, learned with him and became equally adept at controlling the elements.

One night, Nick was lying on his back in the clearing and gazing up at the moon, which was always full in Celestia. "No, Nick," said Mastis, reading his thoughts. "You do not have stewardship over the sun, the moon, or the stars. They are not ours to command. You can form a cloud to shade you from the sun or part the trees to allow the moon to light your path, but that is all you can control."

Nick had become accustomed to Mastis's ability to know what he was thinking, but it never ceased to be a bit intimidating. "Are you going to teach me how to do that?" said Nick, changing the subject.

"Read the thoughts of others? Oh, yes, but communicating with our thoughts will come when you have become stronger and developed more control over both your mind and your heart."

Feelings of frustration filled Nick's heart. He felt like he was strong enough to do anything. Sometimes it seemed that Mastis took forever to teach him each new concept and skill.

Mastis, hearing Nick's thoughts said, "You want to reap before you have sewn and pluck before you have pruned. You must learn that each ability takes both time and patience to develop."

"I'm sorry, Mastis," said Nick, quickly repenting. "I will trust your judgment."

Each morning, Nick hopped on Jazz's back and cantered to the schooling meadow. If they arrived before Mastis, they relaxed by galloping around the perimeter of the meadow. Each time they approached the stream, Jazz leapt from one bank to the other, clearing the water by several feet in height and width. This always made Nick laugh with delight as he gripped Jazz's sides with his legs and held onto Jazz's mane. Sometimes they wove in and out of the tall columns that supported the animal statues. As they did so, the statues followed their movements and cheered them on. Yet, as soon as Mastis arrived, all playing stopped and the serious training began anew.

On this particular day, the always prompt Mastis was late. Nick and Jazz kept up their play until they saw him enter the meadow on the opposite side of the stream. Jazz turned quickly and cantered across the meadow, taking one last leap over the water and stopping just on the other side of the stream bed.

His head came up and his ears pricked straight forward. Nick looked between Jazz's ears. Mastis was not alone.

Following behind the elegant dapple-gray unicorn was what appeared to be a sparkling cloud that seemed to pulsate as it expanded and contracted. When Mastis and his company drew closer, Nick realized that the sparkling cloud was made up of many little bird-like beings. Once Mastis stopped in front of Nick and Jazz, the winged creatures arranged themselves all around the unicorn and hovered in midair.

They were not birds at all, but the fairies Nick had seen on his trip to meet the Council. Each fairy was only about eight inches tall with a body that was much like a human's in shape and proportion. Their facial features, however, were much more angular than a human's, their cheek bones sharp, their noses pointed. They were dressed in gowns that reached just above their knees, revealing two thin legs. The gowns were sleeveless, leaving their equally thin arms bare. Each fairy had a tiny belt that drew in the gown at the waist. The belts sparkled with jewels and reminded Nick of the belts that rodeo queens wore during the summertime rodeo in Cheyenne, Wyoming. Extending from their backs were two sets of wings, the top set being slightly larger than the bottom. The fairies' hair and bodies were several different colors. Some were pink, others yellow. Some were white, others were blue or pale green.

"Good morning, Nicholas and Jazz," said Mastis with a smile on his face. "As you are aware, I have brought some friends with me to help with your training today. These are the fairies of Celestia. They have many important responsibilities in the land behind the mist. They are assigned to be the messengers that go back and forth through the mist to check on the welfare of the animals on Earth. They return and report to the Council when they see an animal that is in need of our assistance. Of most importance to us today, however, is that they hold the keys to the healing powers. Their responsibility is to confer those keys to our foals when they have progressed far enough in their training." Here, Mastis paused. He looked around him at each of the fairies and two of them floated forward.

"I am Gidoni and this is Junia," said one of the two fairies in a tiny voice. "We have been given the responsibility to determine when a foal is ready and worthy to receive these great powers. Our concern has been that you, Nicholas, are obviously not a horse. We have never conferred the healing keys on an immortal human before. So, it has been harder for us to determine if you are worthy. We have been watching your training carefully these many days. We have just returned from visiting with Urijah and the Council. They feel confident that you are ready for this added responsibility."

Junia, looking a bit stern, interjected in a squeaky voice, "I don't mind telling you that I am quite concerned about this whole state of affairs. We really have no precedent upon which to base this decision as you are the first human to progress this far in your training. The last time a human was here was not a good experience for any of us."

"Junia, that is not our concern now. You cannot judge Nicholas by the actions of another. Besides, the Council has made their decision," said Mastis, firmly but not unkindly.

"Yes, and I will abide by the decision of the Council." Junia, duly chastised, moved back a bit and bowed her head toward Mastis. "You are right, Mastis. Our job is not to question; our job is to obey."

Gidoni fluttered his pale-green wings and moved through the air until he was at eye level in front of the two students. He remained in place with his wings moving as fast as a hummingbird's. "Nicholas and Jazz, as Mastis has told you, we hold the keys to the healing powers. These powers can only be used for good. As you have displayed a desire to serve the Animal Kingdom in all ways that are noble and great, we have been asked to pass these powers to you as we have done throughout time to the unicorns."

He stopped for a moment and looked deeply into each of their eyes, dwelling on Nick's for a long time. Feeling the fairy's power penetrating his body, Nick shivered.

"There are many types of injuries in the mortal world," Gidoni continued. "There are injuries of the body, both internal and external, and there are injuries of the heart and mind. The latter are often the hardest to diagnose and to heal. We can give you the power to heal all of these injuries, but you must realize that healing the injuries of the heart and mind takes a tremendous amount of love. This work is exhausting and may take a long time as well. You will find that patience is a virtue that you will want to cultivate to a greater degree than you currently have," he said, looking at Nick.

After what seemed to Nick to be a long time, Gidoni's eyes let go of their hold on Nick and he turned toward Mastis. "Mastis is a master healer. He used the power we gave him to heal both of you. He truly is your savior," Gidoni said with a smile. "We were very proud of his work."

Mastis acknowledged the compliment with a smile and a slight nod of his head.

"We will now begin the Healing Arts Ceremony," said Gidoni.

At that, Mastis stepped back and all of the fairies moved into a circle around Nick and Jazz. The fairies began flying around them with their wings moving so quickly that they were a blur of color. They began chanting in a language that Nick could not understand. Yet the words were rhythmic and beautiful, the way the Italian language sounds to an American.

The fairies' bodies began pulsating with light in response to the cadence of the chant. One by one the fairies left the moving circle and flew over Nick and Jazz. As they did so, they placed their hands on the foals' heads and a glimmer of light penetrated through Nick's and Jazz's bodies. Once each fairy passed power into Nick and Jazz, that fairy's body ceased pulsating light, and Nick's and Jazz's bodies increased in brightness by a proportionate amount. This was a slow and complex process, as each of the dozens of fairies took their turn imbuing Nick and Jazz with the healing powers they possessed. Once the last fairy fulfilled her duty, the fairies moved back and the musical chanting stopped.

"You now have all of the powers to heal that we possess. Only the ancient fairy Animara holds more power. Use them for good or they will be taken away from you," reminded Gidoni. "Nicholas, you will use your hands to be instruments of healing. Jazz, once you have earned your horn, you will use that to heal others. For the time being, use your great powers of concentration."

Jazz bowed in acknowledgement of the instructions just received.

Junia flew forward. As she drew closer, Nick noticed that her tiny face was very beautiful. Her miniature eyes sparkled as she smiled. "Nicholas, I want to tell you that I feel much more confident now. When I placed my hands upon your head, I could feel the power within you. You will do great things for the animals and I am grateful that I have been able to do my small part to help you."

Nick bowed before her. "Thank you, Junia. I promise you that I will not disappoint you."

"I know that you won't."

With these parting words, the fairies left the meadow like an effervescent cloud. Not until then did Nick and Jazz notice that they had another visitor in the schooling arena. Nick wondered if perhaps Mastis had been aware of their visitor's presence long before he was.

Mastis turned toward the unicorn that stood silently on the edge of the schooling arena. With that silent acknowledgment, Helam stepped forward. "Greetings, Nicholas and Jazz. I bring the love of Urijah and the Council of the Twelve Ancients. We remain your humble servants," he said with a bow.

Jazz and Mastis welcomed Helam with the customary unicorn greeting and Nick bowed.

"Now, please tell me how you are feeling about your training."

Nick and Jazz excitedly responded with a recount of all the things Mastis had been teaching them. With each account, Helam nodded approvingly. They concluded with the Healing Arts Ceremony and Helam smiled. "Yes, I was privileged to observe that important event. Now, tell me, Nicholas. You have a question for the Council that has been weighing heavily upon your heart and mind."

Nick, suddenly feeling timid, looked down at his bare feet. Now aware that Helam could read his thoughts, he wondered why it was necessary for him to voice his concern.

"I cannot help you unless you ask," responded Helam to his thoughts.

Taking a deep breath for added confidence, Nick looked up at the beautiful and kind unicorn. "I worry about my family. Will I ever see them again?"

Helam stepped up to Nick. The unicorn rubbed his muzzle along Nick's cheek, infusing him with a feeling of peace and comfort. "The time will come, but not until you have completed your training. You will then have to decide if you want to remain serving the Animal Kingdom or if you want to go to the Human Kingdom. We, of the Council of the Twelve Ancients, realize that this has been both a difficult and wonderful time for you and that your decision will not come easily. We trust that, once you are fully prepared, you will make the correct decision. As to whether you will see your family again, we will make sure that happens before you make your decision."

A warm wave of energy went through Nick's entire body and he turned and threw his arms around Jazz's neck. A bit embarrassed about his response, he turned back to Helam. "Thank you, Helam. Those words give me the strength to carry on and complete my training."

"We will continue to observe your progress. Remember, we are here to serve you." The unicorn bowed so low that his horn touched the ground. Then, he arose, turned, and cantered out of the meadow. The three friends were left alone to contemplate the events of the day.

~ chapter 8 ~

an Uninvited Guest

Nick felt both overwhelmed and excited as a result of all that had occurred during the day. As he and Jazz walked back through the darkening woods toward their home in the clearing, he marveled at the light that radiated from their bodies. Their light illuminated the trees and bushes around them for several feet in every direction. As he watched the glow move ahead of his steps, he thought about the many ways he might be asked to use his power to heal. Would he, one day, be able to save another person or accompany them into immortality as Mastis and Shema had done for him and Jazz? Would the Council ever send him on a mission through the mist to help an injured animal? Would he and Jazz be allowed to work as a team as they did now? Had anyone or any*thing* gone to help his family when they were fatally injured? He still had so much to learn, and that realization was humbling.

Nick reached over and stroked Jazz on his neck as they walked along. He wondered what the big Hanoverian horse was thinking. He smiled to himself as he thought about Gidoni's counsel to him about developing the virtue of patience. He had never been patient with himself. In his Earth life, he had always been pushing himself to succeed, to do better in school, to become a better rider or faster skier. He set lofty goals for himself and worked hard to accomplish them. However, when it came to working with animals, and especially horses, he had always considered himself very patient. In fact, Nick's patience was what motivated Jazz to bond with him so quickly after they first started working together during their Earth life.

In the beginning of his immortal life, Nick knew he had not been patient. He wanted to learn everything immediately and not go through Mastis' prescribed progression. He found that humility helped him develop patience and he appreciated Mastis' occasional chastisement to "sew before you reap and prune before you pluck." This virtue just didn't come naturally for him as it seemed to for Jazz.

Lost in these thoughts, he was surprised when they arrived at their cottage. Just as they began to go through the doorway, Jazz stopped suddenly, his nostrils flaring and ears pointing straight forward.

Nick patted Jazz's tense, arched neck and looked at him quizzically. "What's the matter, Jazz?"

"There is something in our cottage with which I am not familiar."

Nick found it strange to feel his heart start pounding so strongly. Except for missing his family, and some feelings of impatience, he had not felt any sensations but love and warmth since he had arrived in Celestia. "What should we do?"

"We have no power if we have fear. Replace your fear with love. When you are ready, we will greet our visitor."

Nick slid off Jazz's back and consciously drew upon the power within him. He felt the fear leave his body. He stepped into his room and looked around. His glowing body lit the room and he let his eyes move from one part of the room to another, looking for whatever Jazz had sensed. Behind him, he heard Jazz move into his stall. The big horse let out a loud snort and a stomp of his hoof. Nick turned and ran into Jazz's part of the cottage. He found Jazz poised and standing firmly on all four legs, his head and neck lowered and outstretched toward a bulge in the straw that covered the floor of his stall. The straw was rustling as whatever was underneath quivered.

Nick and Jazz stepped forward to the mound together. Nick felt no fear, only power as he reached his hand toward the straw. Jazz moved his muzzle forward at the same time. Nick brushed aside some straw just as Jazz blew some away with his hot breath.

At that, whatever had formed the mound burst up and scurried toward the wall, sending straw in all directions. Once the creature reached the wall it turned to face them. Nick blinked and stood up straight as he looked into the dark and terrified eyes of a human girl.

The first thing beyond the eyes that Nick noticed about her was how dark she was. Unlike Nick and all the unicorns, her skin did not radiate any light of its own. The next thing he noticed was how beautiful she was. Her face, though unwashed, was oval in shape. Her eyes were large and set wide apart. Her hair was long and fell in uncombed waves around her face and past her shoulders. She had probably been a few years younger than he was when she had left her Earth life. A ragged, rough looking tunic covered her thin body to her knees. Her feet were bare.

She leaned against the wall and gripped the stones, digging her dirty short fingernails into the crevasses as if she desired to scale a rock face. She looked at them with a face reflecting both fear and defiance.

"Do not be afraid," said Nick, mustering up the calmest-sounding voice he could. "We will not harm you."

The girl did not move nor respond as she stared at him with terror in her eyes.

"Who are you? Do you have a name?" added Jazz calmly.

The girl took her eyes off Nick for the first time and looked at Jazz. Slowly, she seemed to relax just a bit as she looked at the beautiful horse.

"You are not a unicorn," she said in a whisper to Jazz. "You are a very beautiful horse."

"Thank you, my dear," replied Jazz lovingly. "You are a very beautiful girl. My name is Jazz. What is your name?"

Obviously feeling more comfortable talking to Jazz than Nick, she looked down and shyly responded, "My name is Bethany."

"Bethany," uttered Nick in a whisper.

She jerked her head up and looked at Nick, the fear back in her eyes.

"We will not hurt you. Can you tell us why you are here?"

Bethany glared at him and did not respond, so Nick tried again. "Are you hungry? What can we do for you? Do you need our help?"

"You cannot help me!" She nearly spit the words at him. Nick looked over at Jazz in frustration.

Jazz took the cue. "Bethany, this is Nicholas. He is my best friend. He can be your friend, too, if you will let him."

"I have no friends. I am not worthy of friends," responded the girl with both sadness and anger in her voice.

"Please, come sit on the bed and let us talk to you," said Jazz as he stepped up to the girl and caressed her cheek with his soft muzzle.

The girl seemed to melt at Jazz's touch and she put both her hands on either side of his big head and stroked his cheeks. Jazz stood still and silent for several minutes while she looked into his dark, sparkling eyes with her equally dark but dull ones. She placed the index finger of her right hand on his forehead and traced the double cowlicks. "My horse had a double cowlick," she said in a whisper so low that Nick barely caught her words. She looked into the dark, liquid eyes of the horse, gave a tiny nod of her head and the three, with Nick in the lead, walked into Nick's part of the cottage.

Jazz led Bethany to the edge of the bed and gently pushed her with his head. Nick approached her slowly and offered her a cup of milk and a crispy roll. She looked up with panic in her eyes before she snatched the food from his hands and ravenously consumed the bread and gulped down the milk.

For several minutes, Nick and Jazz stood in front of Bethany while she ate. After she shoved the last bit of roll into her mouth and drank the last of the milk, she wiped her mouth with the back of her hand and let out a long sigh. Only then did she look up at Nick. He was relieved to see some softening in her countenance. "Thank you," she said sweetly and dropped her eyes.

"What are you doing here?" asked Nick tenderly.

Bethany immediately tensed and pulled back farther onto the bed.

Nick turned the conversation over to Jazz once again. "Do not worry, little one. You have nothing to fear from us. You can tell us why you are here."

In a whisper, Bethany responded, "Hasbadana sent me." Her body shivered as she spoke the name of the Lord of the Dark Kingdom.

The pieces suddenly fell into place for Nick. This was the girl who had been brought into Celestia. This was the girl he had heard about from the Council and the fairies. "Why did he send you to us?"

"He didn't send me *to* you. He sent me to spy on you. He wants to know what you have been trained to do. He wants to know what powers you have been given. I have been watching you for a long time. You see, I have none of your powers. This makes Hasbadana livid. He thinks that humans can never be as powerful as the unicorns so he wants to know what you are capable of." She paused, and slowly, hesitantly continued. "The unicorns are kind to you here in Celestia, perhaps because you are so powerful. The unicorns that guard me are not so kind," she said and her eyes lowered to her hands that were clutched together in her lap, her knuckles white.

"You have the same power that I do, Bethany; you just haven't had the same teachers that I have had."

"No, I don't and I never will. I hear them talking about love. They tell you to draw upon the love that you have within you to develop your power. I don't have any love within me. The only thing that ever loved me was my horse, Lady…I mean, Shema."

At the mention of that name, both Nick and Jazz started. "You mean Shema was the horse that brought you here?"

"Yes, but she is a unicorn now, so even she wouldn't love me anymore."

"Oh, Bethany, you are wrong. As a unicorn, she is now capable of loving you even more than she did before," insisted Nick.

"No, Hasbadana told me that she never wants to see me again."

"He is the father of lies." said Jazz with bitterness in his voice.

"Hasbadana doesn't lie. He knows all things. He especially knows all about me. I am lucky that he even gives me a home to live in," she said as her dark eyes welled up with tears.

Suddenly the sound of unicorn hoofbeats was heard outside the cottage door. Nick and Jazz turned to look and, as they did so, they heard a pain-filled scream from Bethany.

They turned just in time to see the young girl being sucked into the darkness.

In an instant, she was gone. But the look of pain and panic in her eyes just before she disappeared burned a lasting impression on Nick's mind.

Mastis and Shema hurried into Nick's room. "She was here! Oh, my little Bethany was here!" exclaimed Shema.

"We have arrived too late, Shema, I'm so sorry," said Mastis as he rubbed his cheek against her in comfort. Turning to Nick and Jazz, he continued. "We heard your thoughts and hurried here as fast as we could. I wish we could have arrived in time to help her."

"Oh, Mastis, she is so filled with darkness," said Nick as he went up to the unicorn and hugged his neck.

"Yes, she didn't come to Celestia with all of the love that you brought with you. I will let Shema tell you the story." With that, he turned and looked at Shema, who stood beside him with her head down and glistening tears streaming from her eyes. Even in her time of sorrow, she sparkled like a diamond and filled the room with beautiful light, just the opposite of the darkness that Bethany had brought with her.

After a short time, Shema composed herself and began her story. "Bethany was born in the place called Colorado to a mother who was not happy that she came to her. She was always angry and took out her resentment on Bethany. Sometimes she yelled at her, sometimes she hit her, but all of the time she told her how much she hated her and wanted her dead. Bethany had one escape in her life: horses. From the time she was little she had a love for horses. As a young child she pretended to be a horse. She cantered around her living room and whinnied like a horse, until her mother came home and made her be silent. One day, when Bethany was nine years old, her kind neighbors noticed her pretending to be a horse.

They asked her mother if they could take her to visit a youth riding club called The Westernaires to see if they would let her ride with them. Her mother was all too glad to have Bethany 'out of her hair.' The Westernaires take children from Jefferson County, Colorado, and teach them how to ride, regardless of their ability to pay for the lessons. Many kind adults help the children learn to ride and care for horses. As the children become better riders, they are allowed to perform in their drill team. My, my, all of this is a grand time for horses and children. Ah, yes, a grand time." added Shema with a sparkle in her eyes. "But, as usual, I am going off on a tangent," she said with a smile.

"I was one of the horses owned by the Westernaires. My name in my Earth life was Lady. Bethany was assigned to be my caregiver and, in turn, I helped her learn how to ride. Bethany never missed a day coming to my stable. She cleaned the neighbor's house to earn bus fare to ride to the barn from her apartment in Lakewood. She became an excellent rider and became my best friend. We were together for six years. We loved each other just as you and Jazz love each other, Nicholas."

Shema stopped her narration for a moment to blink a tear from her eye. "One day," she continued, "after a grand performance at the National Western Stock Show in Denver, a man came to our stable. He paid our director a large sum of money to purchase me for his daughter. My heart was breaking when they came to load me into the horse trailer. Indeed, my heart was breaking. I panicked at the thought of never seeing Bethany again. I whinnied and whinnied, calling out for her. I refused to walk into the horse trailer for quite a while. Finally, exhausted from my struggle, I stepped slowly into the trailer. The men latched the rear doors of the trailer, trapping me inside."

Shema blinked away another tear. "No sooner did the trailer start to move than I saw the city bus stop in front of the stable. Out stepped Bethany. I admit I panicked once again. I whinnied and kicked. I bucked and reared in the trailer. Bethany heard my cries for help and ran down the street after us, crying out 'Lady! Lady!' I broke off my halter and kicked open the back door of the trailer. As the trailer went around a curve in the road, I fell out onto the pavement. I was badly hurt and could not stand up. Bethany was soon at my head, holding me. At that moment, I looked up to see a large truck bearing down on us. That is all I remember until I awoke in Celestia with my savior, Helam, standing over me."

Here, Shema sighed loudly, and Mastis rubbed her neck with his muzzle. She looked over at him with a smile.

"Helam told me that I had refused to come with him without Bethany. So, he brought my best friend here as well, even though bringing a human to Celestia had never been done before. He healed her of all her injuries. However, it took quite a long time. You see, she did not have enough love in her to draw upon. Before the Council could decide what to do with her, Hasbadana and his followers took her to the Dark Kingdom."

Shema started to cry. "I do not believe that she went by choice. I firmly believe that she was stolen away from us against her will."

"Why didn't you go save her?" asked Nick.

"I had already become a unicorn and unicorns cannot go into the Dark Kingdom. Our responsibility is here in the light of Celestia, in the Animal Kingdom and helping the animals on Earth. But not a day has gone by that I have not thought of her. When Mastis heard through your thoughts that you were talking to her, I came as fast as I could…but, alas, we were too late. He has taken her back. Oh, me, oh my. He has taken her back!" Her tears came harder this time.

Nick sat silently, looking from Shema to Mastis to Jazz. His thoughts moved rapidly and in a disorganized manner, but one theme prevailed: he and Jazz were not unicorns...they could go into the Dark Kingdom.

Even though Mastis could read Nick's thoughts, there was no response from the big dapple-gray unicorn.

chapter 9

Dreams

The dreams started that night, or perhaps it should be said, that morning, as it was not far from sunrise when Mastis and Shema left, and Jazz and Nick attempted to sleep. Nick was restless for the first time in his wonderful down bed, and when he slept he had disturbing dreams that caused him to awaken with perspiration covering his glistening body.

In his dreams, he could just barely make out Bethany's body in the darkness, but she was not alone. There was a unicorn with her. This unicorn reminded him of the "demon horse" at the entrance to the Denver Airport, the metal sculpture of a rearing horse with glowing red eyes. This was the sculpture that fell over and crushed its own creator, the artist Luis Jimenez. The resemblance was not in the color of the body or the eyes but in the sharpness of the angles of his body and the aura of anger and evil that surrounded the creature. Even before he heard Bethany say his name, Nick sensed that this was Hasbadana.

Nick felt that he was actually in the dark room, observing the encounter. More than that, he sensed that he wasn't observing it as a third person but as though he could see through Bethany's eyes. He could feel her fear and despair. He could only have guessed the meaning of these words before. Now he understood the depth of emotion that these expressions attempted to convey. He felt the darkness all around him, no longer using just his eyes. He felt a dense coldness that pained his skin.

Hasbadana's voice did not make lovely melodic sounds like the unicorns he knew. The sound was low and deep and hurt his ears like a dissonant chord in music. He flinched each time the unicorn spoke and Nick desired nothing more than for him to stop talking.

The unicorn never ceased moving as he circled his victim, for victim she was. He was relentless with his disparaging remarks. "I feel only abhorrence when I look at you! To think that you are a member of the human race that feels entitled to rule over all the Earth and Animal Kingdom! Why you sully the name of all humans," he sneered.

"I did my best, Master Hasbadana," came the whispered reply from Bethany.

"*I did my best,*" Hasbadana mocked. "Your best! Is that what you call your best?" He spoke with a sardonic sneer on his face. "You insult my intelligence if you think I would accept that as an explanation. You let them not only find you, but because you are an imbecile, they were able to convince you to tell them why you were there." His harangue continued as he berated her for what he perceived to be her failed mission.

Bethany's thoughts grew darker and colder as she endured the reprimand. After all, she had been the victim of her mother's tongue-lashings all of her mortal life. Her thoughts turned to self-incrimination as she pondered the verbal attacks she had endured. Perhaps her mother and Hasbadana were right after all. She was weak and worthless. Anyone who had ever known her well thought that was the case so it must be true.

"No!" yelled Nick, sitting straight up in bed. He had forced himself awake both to escape the dream and in response to the thoughts that Bethany was conjuring in her head. Nick blinked his eyes and looked around his cottage in the faint pre-dawn light. He felt weak and shaken.

Jazz, awakened by the outburst from his friend, stood in his stall, shook off the straw that stuck to the sides of his body, and walked into Nick's room. "What is the matter, my boy?" he asked Nick soothingly.

"Don't speak out loud, just think something," replied Nick with reservation.

Calmly, Jazz thought about the previous night with Bethany. "I can hear you. I can hear your thoughts," exclaimed Nick. "It wasn't a dream at all. I was hearing Bethany's thoughts in my sleep. She is back in the dark kingdom with Hasbadana. She is so frightened, but more than that, she has given complete credence to Hasbadana's hostile accusations. She is weak because she believes his verbal attacks."

But what can we do with her under his power and influence? asked Jazz silently, intentionally testing Nick's new abilities.

"Remember that the fairies gave us power to heal both the body and the spirit," responded Nick as though Jazz had spoken aloud.

They said that the spirit was the hardest to heal, responded Jazz once again in his thoughts.

Nick was pacing back and forth, now. "I remember, but we must try."

Perhaps we should discuss this with Mastis.

Nick stopped pacing and turned to look at Jazz. *Perhaps we don't need to. Perhaps he already knows what I am thinking,* answered Nick silently.

Jazz smiled at Nick, "So, two can play at this game."

"How long have you been able to hear my thoughts?" asked Nick.

"I developed that ability just a few days ago. I am so glad that we will be able to communicate with our thoughts from now on. I foresee that this ability might come in very handy in the future."

That was only the first of many nights in which Nick was able to share Bethany's thoughts. Hasbadana assailed her daily as he complained about her lack of power. Being informed of Nick's strengths and talents only seemed to anger Hasbadana more. Yet Nick sensed that Hasbadana was perfectly aware that he was the one destroying her power, as though he could feel himself becoming stronger as she became weaker.

Soon, the day came that Hasbadana approached Bethany with a new tone to his rebukes. "You are nothing more than an encumbrance," he said, spitting the words out at her in his deep, menacing voice. Pacing back and forth in front of her, his long flowing tail swishing as he walked, he continued. "I desire to be rid of you. What to do with you, however, has been a difficult decision. I dare not return you to Celestia for you know too much of my plans and have seen too many of my powers and abilities. And I doubt that the Human Kingdom would want you. Therefore, since I desire to have you out of my sight forever, my servants have been instructed to take you to the most distant part of my kingdom where you can never again offend my sensibilities." With that said the dark, angular body of the unicorn turned and left the cold, stone room.

Two of Hasbadana's servants entered the room. In Earth life, they had been beautiful bay Clydesdales, but in the Dark Kingdom, their beauty had been replaced with darkness. Each grabbed one of Bethany's arms with their teeth and lifted her into the air between them. The young girl cried out in pain, a cry that the large unicorns simply ignored. As if on cue, the two dark unicorns galloped out of the room and down a long hallway. Their hooves clattered on the stones and Nick, seeing through Bethany's thoughts, could discern that they were running quickly through a castle-like fortress lit only by an occasional torch mounted to the walls. Once they exited the structure where Bethany had been kept, they continued running.

The outdoor surroundings were in muted grays and blacks, similar to Andrew Wyeth's late period paintings with their lack of vibrant color. All around, the trees seemed like they were dormant, as though in the middle of winter, projecting forth from the ground like the bare bones of the Earth. Not long after these first images were transmitted from Bethany's thoughts to Nick's dream, all went black. Nick had no doubt that the pain of the unicorn's hold on her arms as they carried her in the air between them caused her to escape through unconsciousness.

Nick awoke to find that the dream had lasted through the entire night, and another beautiful morning was about to bless his day. The contrast was startling. He knew he must find a way to save Bethany, save her from both Hasbadana and the past she carried with her.

Mastis arrived in the schooling arena just as Nick and Jazz did. He got right to the point as he was wont to do. "I see that you have made an important decision."

"Yes, Mastis."

"You realize that this will not be an easy, nor comfortable endeavor."

"I realize that."

"And Jazz is in agreement with you." This was said as a statement, not a question but Nick answered anyway.

"He is." Nick said the words even as he turned to look at his beloved horse.

Jazz nodded in agreement. "Nick and I are as one on this."

"Yes, I knew as much. However, you are still foals and have little experience in such matters. Going into the Dark Kingdom is far more difficult than you realize. There are two things that we must do before you undertake such a task. I want to teach you how to become invisible and I want you to receive both permission and a blessing from the Council."

Nick's heart raced within him as he realized that he had just been given authorization to begin his preparations to rescue Bethany. Approval from Mastis was of utmost importance to him. Without it, he doubted that he would have been able to proceed with any kind of plan. Yet feelings of eager anticipation and inadequacy mingled into a swirling pattern in his head. He could hear Jazz's thoughts and knew that his outward confidence belied his feelings as well.

"Follow me," instructed Mastis. Nick swung up onto Jazz's back. The horse, unicorn, and boy galloped out of the circular meadow.

Where are we going, Mastis? asked Nick in his thoughts.

To the highest point in Celestia, was the unspoken reply.

chapter 10

The Quest

Jazz followed Mastis as they galloped through the woods and into the same meadow they had crossed on the day they went to visit the Council. This time, however, just as the cliffs of the Council's chamber came into view, they turned to the right. Ahead of them, on the far edge of the meadow, the ground rose sharply into the air and formed a lush, green mountain. The mountain stood isolated, surrounded on all sides by the flowers and grasses of the meadow. None of the rolling hills or rocky cliffs that Nick had previously seen in Celestia were nearly as tall. A few wispy, white clouds anchored themselves to the peak of the mountain. Jazz and Mastis slowed their gallop first to a canter then to a trot and finally down to a walk as they kept their eyes on the object of their journey.

As they reached the base of the mount, Mastis stopped and turned toward them. "This is Mount Elisia. The mount stands at the center of Celestia. All horses, before they become unicorns, must ascend its slopes alone."

He paused, looking at Nick. Nick responded by sliding off Jazz's back. The Hanoverian was breathing hard and Nick placed his hand on Jazz's muscular neck to comfort his horse.

He could feel the damp perspiration that had resulted from their long ride on the smooth hairs of Jazz's neck. He turned his thoughts back to Mastis.

"You will each take your own path up the mountain," continued Mastis. "As you do so, the skills you have learned will be tested. Once you reach the top, you must find the invisible clover. Pick enough flowers to fill this bag and bring the bag back down with you," Mastis stretched his neck and head toward them. In his mouth he held two small canvas bags with long straps.

Nick reached forward and took the bags. He put the strap of one over Jazz's neck and put his head and one arm through the strap of the other. The strap crossed his chest like a Boy Scout merit badge sash and the little bag rested at his hip. "How are we to find clover that is invisible?" Nick asked.

"You will know the clover when you do not see it," said Mastis.

Nick and Jazz both cocked their heads. It wasn't like Mastis to speak in riddles.

Mastis only smiled. "Enjoy your journey," he said as he turned and looked at the path ahead of them. Nick and Jazz did the same.

Several yards ahead Nick noticed that the path split in two. With an equal measure of confidence and determination, he stepped onto the path. Jazz followed right behind. At the juncture, Nick stopped. Jazz stepped up beside him.

Good luck, my friend, thought Jazz as he blew warm air from his nostrils onto Nick's cheek.

You, too, responded Nick. The two friends parted ways for the first time since they had been in Celestia. Nick turned to the right; Jazz stepped onto the trail that went to the left.

Mastis's last words, "Enjoy your journey," echoed in Nick's head as he stepped along the path with eager anticipation. He was reminded of the family hikes up Longs Peak in Rocky Mountain National Park. He smiled to himself. The trail to the summit of that mountain, one of Colorado's "Fourteeners," so called because Long's Peak was over 14,000 feet in elevation, started out easily as the trail climbed gently through lodge pole pines and aspen groves. However, before he and his family reached the top, the trail became steep and rocky. Nick had only kept going because he didn't want his sisters to best him. *There is that pride again,* he thought to himself with a smile.

He laughed as he heard Jazz respond to his thoughts. *Sometimes pride helps us accomplish great things.*

Or comes just before the fall, Nick responded back. A warm feeling filled his whole being as he realized that, at least for now, he wasn't really alone.

The gentle slope soon gave way to a much steeper trail. After several switchbacks in the trail, Nick paused to catch his breath. He had been climbing steadily for what must have been an hour. He remembered that Mastis had told him his skills would be tested. Yet his only test thus far had been his endurance. He wiped the sweat from his forehead with his sleeve. He could feel his tunic sticking to his back. He rolled his shoulders backwards to find some relief for the stiffness he could feel there. After resting for a few minutes, he continued on. The trail went around a rocky outcropping on the side of the mountain. Nick caught a glimpse of the meadow below and he was surprised at how far up he had come.

He turned back and looked in the direction his feet were taking him and came to an abrupt stop. A mass of several large pines had been uprooted and lay across his path. Their branches were intertwined forming a nearly solid wall of green and brown. Above and below, the hillside was extremely steep. Beyond the tangle of trees was a washed-out section of trail that left a gap of nearly ten feet.

Nick debated the best course of action. He eventually decided to call upon the skills he had been practicing. He summoned the love within him. As he did so, he could feel the power well up inside him. He commanded the fallen trees to construct a bridge over the gap in the trail. With scrapping and rustling, the branches disentangled themselves. The trunks of the trees turned themselves in line with the direction of the trail. They rose up and came crashing down across the break in the trail. Several of the pines lay side by side to produce the base of the bridge. Others arranged themselves on either side of the newly formed bridge but three feet higher, thus making a railing. Branches laced themselves together creating a lovely lattice-work side to the bridge. Any landscape architect would have been pleased to add such a bridge to their garden.

Nick thanked the trees and walked across the bridge, stroking the trunks that formed the hand rails. He had grown to love and appreciate the force of goodness within all the plants and elements. In his Earth life, he had never given them a second thought. Now, as a result of his training with Mastis, he realized how wonderful the spirit in each part of creation really is.

Nick continued on the path as the trail climbed unrelentingly, at times gently, at times steeply. After rounding a bend in the trail, Nick stood at the edge of a deep and swift-moving mountain stream. He stopped at the water's edge and surveyed the situation. The river rushed and bounced over large boulders but, looking both upstream and downstream, there was no sign of a natural bridge as far as he could see. Nick had hoped to find a rock arrangement that would allow him to cross by jumping from rock to rock. Unfortunately, there was no such pattern.

Nick sat beside the path to rest and consider the situation. Both the hike and the use of his power to command the trees had exhausted him. He laid his head back against the long grass and wildflowers that obtained their nourishment from the river and looked up at the beautiful blue sky. "If you look up and see blue sky and pine trees, life is good," his father's words echoed in his head. A smile crossed his face but a feeling of melancholy filled his breast as he remembered the many hikes he had enjoyed with his father. He felt the love in his heart fill his body with renewed strength and the sadness was driven away.

Next he thought of Jazz, on his own journey to find the invisible clover, and he called out to him with his thoughts. There was no response from the dark bay gelding. While he wanted to communicate with Jazz, Nick was unconcerned that he could not hear his thoughts. Mastis had warned them that going alone was part of the quest.

Feeling renewed and refreshed, Nick stood up and once again considered his situation. The power within him gave him the confidence to do what he was going to do next. He walked toward the water's edge and paused for just a moment before stepping forward. At what should have been the moment of contact with the surface of the water, his foot came down on dry ground. The water moved around his foot but didn't touch him. He stepped forward again and looked down to watch the water swirl around him without touching him. He took step after step and the water continued to move around him without so much as brushing his skin. As he stepped farther into the river bed, the water reached higher and higher around his body but still not a drop touched him. He stepped around and over the rocks that lined the riverbed, rocks that were covered with icy-cold water just one step ahead of him. He didn't look back as Lot's wife had in the Bible story, but continued moving toward the far side of the river.

When he placed his foot on the riverbank, he finally turned back to examine the route he had just taken. He could see the trail on the far side as it disappeared into the water at the river's edge. He marveled at the beauty of the wild, rocky-mountain-like stream as it tumbled over and around boulders. He looked down at his dry feet and clothes. "Thank you, river," he said reverently. Nick turned away from the stream and continued on his path.

Not much farther up the trail, Nick noticed a large bird of some kind standing right in the middle of the narrow path. As Nick approached, he recognized the bird as a bald eagle. In their mortal lives, these strong and elegant birds, the national bird of the United States of America, flew down to Colorado in the winter to nest. After hatching and caring for their young, they flew north for the rest of the year. He had seen a live eagle at the wildlife preserve near Denver. He knew they were afraid of humans and could even attack. But that was in Earth life and this was Celestia. Nothing was the same here.

As he approached, the large bird did not fly off, but stood her ground, watching Nick approach. The white hood of feathers on her head glistened in the sun. The dark feathers of her body lay smooth on the side that was facing Nick. Her round, black eyes watched Nick's every movement. She pivoted her body a half turn and Nick could see that the large wing on her right side lay outstretched and motionless as the appendage lay on the ground to the side of the magnificent bird.

With love in his heart for the splendid creature, Nick approached calmly and quietly. He slowly lowered himself to a kneeling position in front of her. He reached out one hand and gently caressed the bird's head. As he stroked the feathers on the eagle's head, his eyes surveyed the damage to the wing. The bird had a compound fracture of the main bone that supported the otherwise strong wing. Nick stopped stroking the white feathers and placed both his hands over the injured wing. He closed his eyes and pictured a perfect wing, a wing that would battle the angry winds and carry its owner up and over the mountaintops.

He felt the healing power that the fairies had given him well up inside of him and concentrate in his hands. An intense light radiated from his fingertips and shot out toward the injury. Nick opened his eyes and focused his thoughts on the injury. The rays of light from his fingers changed colors: first yellow, then orange, red, then purple, and all through the hues of the rainbow. Nick's hands felt extremely, almost excruciatingly, hot, but Nick didn't stop or change his focus until he was sure that the healing was completed.

He pulled his power back within him, folded his arms against his body and tucked his fingers under his arms. He leaned back and observed the enormous bird. All of this time the bird had not moved, and her eyes had remained riveted on Nick. Now the bird turned her head toward her wing. Slowly, cautiously, she lifted her wing. At first, she moved it up and down just a few inches. Carefully, she tested the wing more aggressively. In an almost reverent motion, she folded the wing against her side as though it had never been broken. She turned straight toward Nick. "Thank you, Master Healer. I will always be your servant."

"No, you will not be my servant. You will be my friend."

"So shall it be. My name is Gloforia. You may call for me and I will hear you. I will come to you immediately," responded the eagle. With that, her beak opened and she let out a loud screech and with one powerful stroke of her wings, lifted herself off the ground. She circled once from high in the air, screeching again, then headed for the mountaintop.

Nick remained in his kneeling position and watched her go. He felt quite sad at the loss of her company. He slowly rose to his feet and, with a warm feeling throughout his entire body, started up the trail once again. He had an overwhelming desire to be able to fly like an eagle. Flying would certainly make it easier to reach the top.

Nick stopped to rest several times as he continued to make his way up the mountain. The trail seemed to become steeper and rockier with each switchback as it wove up the side of the peak. He was grateful for the trees that provided shade most of the way and the occasional stump on which he could sit and rest. He enjoyed taking drinks from the cool mountain water that he called up from the ground, and eating fruits and berries that he called forth from the trees and bushes. When night came, he carved a shelter from a large rock, lined the alcove with a bed of pine needles, and covered himself with leaves. His was a dreamless sleep that night.

When he awakened to the melodic song of the morning dove, he was shocked to be greeted with snow covering the ground. This was surprising not only because it was the first snow he had seen in Celestia but also because the air wasn't cold. He had grown up on the East Coast of the United States and knew the biting cold that accompanied a snowfall. But here, near the top of the mountain, he felt like it was a perfect seventy-five-degree day with sunshine encapsulating him and a gentle breeze to brush his skin. Yet, after rubbing his eyes to make sure he wasn't imagining it, he looked again and there was, indeed, snow on the ground.

"I will never learn what to expect in Celestia," he said out loud.

Nick stood and brushed the leaves off his body and out of his hair. He stepped out from under his stone shelter and looked around for his trail. Nothing except the white snow greeted him. The ground and all of the trees and bushes were covered in a deep blanket of warm snow. Nothing in his surroundings looked familiar. He wasn't sure which direction he had come from, nor which direction he should go.

Nick sat cross-legged in the snow and looked around him. He picked up the flakes of snow in handfuls, enjoying the warmth they provided. He brought his hands up and buried his face in the snow, enjoying the sensation. This made him feel remarkably refreshed, as though he had just had a long soak in his pool back at his cottage. Smiling with pleasure, Nick stood up, ready to renew his journey up the mountain. Calling forth the power within him, he commanded the path to show itself. Silently, the sparkling crystals of snow twinkled and melted away along the curving, rocky line of the trail. After expressing his words of thanks, Nick started up the snow-lined path.

The next couple of hours were uneventful as Nick climbed up the mountain trail. He eventually left the trees behind. The snow continued to dissolve along the path in front of him as he hiked, leaving the trail clear and easy to follow. Upon rounding a wide bend in the path, Nick came to an abrupt stop. Ahead of him was a gigantic stone wall extending in both directions until the structure curved out of sight around the bend of the peak. The stones were many shades of brown and gray. Their edges fit tightly together as though placed there by a master craftsman. He looked ahead at the path he was following and saw that it led right up to a high, arched door that was set into the wall. On either side of the door were two life-sized statues of mountain lions poised on top of intricately carved pedestals. Snow was piled on their heads and backs.

"Why do they have to be mountain lions?" Nick asked out loud. "Why not lambs?" He smiled to himself as he tried to picture two guardian lambs on either side of the door. "Yes, that would be much better."

Nick stepped forward cautiously. His heart was pounding though he didn't know what was causing him to feel so much anxiety. He tried to keep picturing lambs, gentle lambs. Without warning, the mountain lions came to life, shook the snow off their bodies and pounced off their pedestals. They landed soundlessly in front of Nick. Their stone eyes, now alive and full of fury, glared at him. Their lips curled back, revealing sharp teeth and fangs. Each stood on three legs with the right front leg lifted like an English pointer hunting dog. Indeed, hunters they were, and Nick appeared to be the hunted.

Nick, who had stopped abruptly the moment the big cats pounced, held his breath as he looked into their flaming eyes. The mountain lion attack that he survived in Rocky Mountain National Park flashed vividly through his mind. Suddenly, his training took over as if by reflex, and he gained control of his thoughts and feelings. *I have not been given the power of fear but of love,* he told himself firmly. He drew his power from deep within his heart and extended his love outward toward the mountain lions. Slowly, quietly, he began walking toward the pair. For a moment, there was no discernable change in the cats' demeanor. Continuing to extend love, Nick stepped forward confidently. As if they functioned as one entity, both cats remained seated and began cleaning their paws; their eyes shifted their focus onto their new task.

Relieved, Nick stepped up to the large cats and rubbed them both behind their ears. They stopped their grooming ritual and rubbed the sides of their heads against Nick's body. Nick spoke soothingly to each of them as he stroked their yellow fur.

As Nick caressed the great cats, he looked ahead at the door. The ingress was nearly fifteen feet tall and rounded at the top. Three iron bars with heavy studs held the planks of wood together. Bronze hinges held the door tightly shut. A large doorknob was attached to the right side of the door. No keyhole or lock was visible. Carved into the stone over the door were unfamiliar symbols. Nick realized that this could be the written form of the unicorn's language, a language he could now speak and understand but had never seen in written form. Nick left the mountain lions, stepped up to the door, and took a hold of the black iron doorknob. He attempted to turn the knob but it would not move. He placed both hands on the door and pushed, but once again, the lock did its job: the door did not budge. He took a step back and examined the door carefully.

He turned back toward the mountain lions. "Do you know how I can open this door?" Nick asked them, hoping he had earned their trust.

Both lions looked up and responded in unison, "The instructions are written over the door." As though they had never been interrupted, they went back to grooming themselves.

Nick turned his eyes up to look again at the strange symbols written over the arched doorframe.

ακ δγτχ αφσγη δωφ η϶γη φσ ηφθυ

He tried to make sense out of them. They were so unfamiliar; he couldn't even tell how many words they represented.

Nick searched his brain to try to figure out the best way to unlock this mystery. He kneeled down and started writing in the sand in front of the door. The letters he wrote were in English, a language he hadn't used since he had arrived in Celestia. He smiled when he read the word he had written: LOVE. Suddenly, the answer came to him. He took his hand and brushed away the letters he had been writing. He stood up, facing the door. Lifting his eyes to look at the symbols over his head, and drawing the power from within him, he commanded: "Change your shape into letters from the English language."

With a scratching sound, the shapes began to move and alter their form. Within a few minutes, the stone carvings that had been so foreign to him now stood out clearly in letters from the English alphabet.

KNOCK AND IT SHALL BE OPENED UNTO YOU

"Thank you," Nick replied.

Immediately the letters returned to their original shapes. Nick stepped up to the heavy, studded door and knocked. The door slowly swung open on its bronze hinges with a loud groan.

~ chapter 11 ~

Invisible Clover

The door opened into a vast dome-shaped field of clover, not your typical mountain summit, but Nick reminded himself this was Celestia. The field was filled with clover leaves and flowers crowding each other tightly together, which reminded Nick of the field of poppies in *The Wizard of Oz*. He stepped gently onto the green and pink carpet and noticed that he stood on top of the flowers without crushing them.

Nick was startled by the loud bang of the door slamming shut behind him. He looked back quickly and saw that there was no doorknob on this side. His gaze drifted to the top of the doorway and he noticed symbols carved into the stone on this side of the wall similar to the ones that had been carved on the other side. He hoped they were the same instructions: *Knock and it shall be opened unto you.* Yet, he had a sinking feeling that they were different.

Nick turned his attention back to the meadow. He backed up until he was leaning against the stone wall. He placed his hands against the rough stone to steady himself as the enormity of his challenge weighed upon him. There, spread in all directions in front of him, was an entire mountaintop covered with clover. But the problem that manifested itself was that all of these flowers were as visible as Nick himself although without his sparkling skin. How would he ever find invisible flowers? *This was going to be harder than finding Waldo in a candy cane factory,* he thought.

"Well, I guess I had just better get started," Nick said aloud. He stepped away from the wall and marveled again that the flowers and leaves were able to support his weight as he walked on them. He instinctively headed toward the top of the dome, hoping that the vantage point from the top would give him some sort of an added advantage. When he arrived at the summit, however, he was able to see that the entire dome was a carpet of flowers in all directions. No area looked any different than any other.

Nick sat down cross-legged on the top of the mountain. He reached in front of him and picked a flower, twirling it between his fingers. He stopped twisting the flower and began carefully studying it. The stem was several inches long. Attached to the stem was the characteristic leaf made up of three leaflets, which were the reason for its scientific name: trifoliate. At the top of the stem was the head, or flower. The colorful blossom was made up of dense spikes. The bottom spikes were dark pink while the upper spikes decreased in the amount of pigment until the top spikes were white. Nothing seemed unusual about this flower, so Nick tossed it aside and picked another and another and another, tossing each aside until he had a pile of discarded flowers all around him.

"Is this another test of my patience?" Nick yelled out loud. He stopped and listened but nothing answered him. "Mastis, can you hear me?" he tried again. No answer. He stood up and began kicking flowers in all directions as though his foot was a sickle. After clearing an area several feet across, his frustration left him as quickly as it had come and he sat back down on the same spot, though now the carpet of flowers no longer cushioned his body. He wiped the perspiration off of his forehead with his sleeve and looked around at the visible evidence of his temper tantrum. Feelings of shame welled up inside of him. Had he not progressed at all during his time in Celestia? Was he no better a person now than when he had left his Earth life, even with all the training he had received? These thoughts rushed through his head until, with great effort, he was able to send them on their way. He had a source of power within him. He needed to remember to call upon that power if he wanted to be able to overcome his weaknesses.

Nick looked around him with new eyes. Instead of feeling overwhelmed as before, he had a new feeling of confidence. First he drew upon his power and commanded the clover to spring forth from the ground until the destruction he had caused was no longer visible under new, beautiful, and strong clover leaves and flowers. He laughed aloud as he felt the flowers beneath him actually raise him up off the ground as they grew.

In a quiet, reverent voice he spoke aloud to the flowers around him. "I am sorry that I behaved so poorly. I am trying to overcome my weaknesses but I have learned that progress doesn't happen all at once and I still have a long way to go. I hope you will forgive me and that you are willing to help me."

He paused for a moment before continuing. "I have been sent here by Mastis, the great and wise unicorn, to find the invisible clover that I can use to become invisible myself. I pledge to you that I will only use this power for good. I would appreciate it if you would show me the invisible clover that grows in your midst." Nick finished his plea and listened.

"If one listens carefully enough, one can hear a bird sing in the middle of Times Square," his wise grandmother had once told him. She continued with the additional counsel: "One could also hear a coin drop; it just depends upon what is most important to you." Nick felt the power well up inside of him as his heart filled with love. The power felt warmer than usual and he felt peace.

Nick continued to patiently listen, confident that an answer was forthcoming. The sun moved silently down the slope of the flower-covered dome and his shadow lengthened. Subsequently a new shadow moved across the clover. Nick watched the dark shape approach and, as it drew closer to him, he looked up. There in the sky, not far above him, Gloforia the eagle was gracefully and powerfully gliding toward him.

The magnificent eagle landed silently on top of the clover directly in front of him. "Greetings my friend," said the raptor. "I sensed your frustration, but needed to wait until you were in a more peaceful place before approaching you." If eagles could smile, then surely Gloforia was smiling at Nick.

Nick smiled back, half-ashamed that his behavior had been observed and half-proud that he had been able to overcome his weakness. "I'm so glad to have your company, Gloforia, and that you appear to be healed so completely."

The large eagle looked down at her now-perfect wing and stretched it out to show her healer his handiwork. "You have blessed me with your talents and I have come to bless you with mine. My eyesight is very keen and I am able to see even the invisible clover in broad daylight. I sense, however, that it is more important for your schooling that you find the clover yourself. If you will sit here and wait for the darkness, the magical clover will make itself known to you."

The peace that Nick had felt overpowered the feelings of discouragement that wanted to well up inside of him once again. *How can darkness help me find something that is invisible?* he wondered. But the warm feelings filled his soul again as he replaced his discouragement and doubts with trust in the kindness and wisdom of the eagle. "As you say, Gloforia. I will wait for the darkness."

Nick and Gloforia sat silently on the clover as the sun dropped out of sight. Nick was glad for her company. Once the sun had set, Nick watched the sky as it changed from pinks and oranges to grays and dark blues. Eventually blackness filled the ceiling above them and stars began their welcoming twinkle.

"Look, my boy," said Gloforia in a whisper.

Nick let his eyes focus in the darkness and all across the surface of the mountaintop, twinkling like the stars he had been watching above him, were tiny specks of light. Nick looked at the magnificent eagle with wonder. "Are those the invisible clover?"

Gloforia gave a brief nod with her head and her eyes blinked slowly.

Nick unfolded his legs and stood up. He took a few steps forward, reached down and picked the stem that supported one of the sparkling points of light. Bringing the stem close to his face, he could see that the twinkling light seemed to come from nothing at all. As he hesitantly reached forth his finger and touched the light, he realized that there was indeed something solid from which the luminosity was emanating. Nick looked around him. All across this meadow on the top of Mount Elisia, tiny specks of light twinkled. Nick reached around his back and pulled out the bag that Mastis had given him. He put his first stem reverently into the bag and smiled as he watched the light illuminate the inside of the bag. He smiled at his own hand as his skin glowed in the darkness. With a feeling of excitement, he set about filling his bag with the flowers that were no longer invisible to him.

Morning came quickly on the mountaintop. Nick's bag was filled to bulging after his night's work of gathering. How long it had taken him to fill his bag was hard to tell, but Nick had slept the last few hours and now felt refreshed and renewed.

Gloforia bid her farewell at first light and Nick summoned a breakfast of berries, rolls, and honey, using his now-refined skills of command. After eating, Nick opened his bag and removed one of his clover stems. He carefully studied the product of his quest. In the daylight he could no longer see a twinkling light at the top of the six-inch stem. He touched the space where a flower should be and his sensitive fingertips could feel its presence. He brought the invisible clover to his nose. He could smell the sweet fragrance of the clover. But, try as he might, he could not see anything except the clover field beyond. Only his sense of sight tried to deny the existence of the flower. His other senses confirmed the magical flower's presence.

As he examined the stem, he noticed a significant difference between this stem and the others that grew all around him. Unlike the pattern of three leaflets in a cluster that the other clover stems contained, this stem supported groups of four leaves. Nick smiled; he was reminded of the hours spent on his stomach in Central Park in New York searching through patches of clover, looking for four-leaf clovers and the good luck they were supposed to bring him. Now he had a whole bag full of them and they were more powerful than he ever suspected when he was a child.

Nick carefully placed this clover stem back into his bag and stood up. He looked around the walled-in meadow for the arched doorway. Seeing the entryway down the hill behind him, he turned and jogged down the slope, running lightly on top of the flowers. At the doorknob-less door he glanced up once more at the writing in the stone.

ϖτξγφρ ψδφγκ υρφκι τυιοκχ

He hoped the message was the same. Just to be sure, he once again commanded the letters to change into his familiar English and marveled as the letters reformed themselves. With a stab of disappointment Nick read the message:

SEEK AND YE SHALL FIND

Why can't anything be easy around here? he thought. He looked down at his feet and contemplated the new message. *Seek and ye shall find...seek and ye shall find.* He ran the words over and over through his mind. He had learned, upon attempting to enter, that the door required more from him than just a command. With confidence in his ability, he stepped up to the door.

He ran his hands over the rough log planks. Finding nothing that seemed to help, he continued seeking by examining the stone archway that framed the door. At first inspection, he found nothing that seemed to be helpful. Eventually, however, he noticed a beautiful butterfly land on a stone just to the right above his head. He watched the insect with a sense of wonder as it opened and closed its multi-colored and patterned wings three times. Folding its wings together, the butterfly walked on its thin legs toward a gap between the stone and the door frame and disappeared into a dark opening that Nick had not noticed before. He reached his hand up and, with some hesitation, slid his fingers into the space. The stone felt cold to his touch and slightly damp but rather than the rough surface he had expected to find, the stones on both sides felt smooth.

When he had inserted his hand up to his wrist, one of his fingers touched a round button-like object. Without hesitation, he pushed it. Nick quickly pulled back his hand as the large plank door scraped open. With joy and excitement in his heart, he stepped through the doorway and onto the trail that led him back down the mountain.

~ chapter 12 ~

The Council's Blessing

N ick arrived at the base of the mountain late in the afternoon to find Mastis and Jazz waiting for him. Jazz trotted up to him and Nick swung his leg up and over the big gelding's back. He leaned forward over the crest of Jazz's neck and stroked the soft hair. Jazz turned his head and nuzzled his shoulder. "When did you arrive back?" Nick inquired.

"Last night."

"I'm sure glad that this wasn't a race or I would have lost." Nick laughed. "How did you do? Were you successful?"

"Yes, I was successful in completing my assignment," responded Jazz. "Because my eyes are on the side of my head, they were able to pick up the twinkling of the invisible clover as the light bounced off the other blossoms."

By this time, Mastis had joined them and he heard Nick's next question. "Why didn't I see you in the meadow?"

Mastis answered the question: "You both had your own journeys."

"What do you mean by that, Mastis?" asked Nick.

"You both had different challenges to face in order that you might be tested and learn to overcome your weaknesses.

Nick, you had to learn more patience. Jazz, you had to learn to appreciate your strengths."

Nick chuckled, while giving Jazz a firm pat on the neck. "How do you like that, old buddy? I had to learn about my deficiencies and you had to learn about your strengths."

"Do not be concerned," interjected Mastis. "Both strengths and weaknesses can become tools for personal growth if you use them wisely. You have each been successful on your individual quests. I am exceptionally proud of you both." Mastis bowed before them, letting his glowing horn touch the ground.

The three hurried back to the schooling meadow. The unicorn and the horse galloped with amazing speed and each stride covered a tremendous amount of ground. Nick held on to Jazz's mane and squeezed his eyes closed as they practically flew through the forest. Though it had never happened, Nick was still afraid that they would hit the trees as they ran by them. Occasionally, Nick opened one eye and peeked at the trail they were speeding along. To his relief, he noticed that the trees in their path actually moved out of their way as they sped by. Nick drew forth enough courage to look behind them and he noticed that the trees resumed their original positions once the little group was out of the way. Slowly, Nick summoned the courage to keep his eyes open and watched the trees zoom by as they galloped past them.

They arrived in the schooling meadow just as the sun set. The animal statues seemed to dance in celebration of their return. Shema and several of the unicorns that the two foals had come to know were awaiting their arrival with another feast. "Eating like a horse," the common human phrase, continued to apply to the immortal unicorns.

Once all the food was consumed, Mastis excused all their friends except Shema.

"Let us teach them how to use the invisible clover they have gathered," said Mastis to the sparkling unicorn.

"That would be a marvelous idea," responded Shema with her characteristic enthusiasm.

"Nicholas and Jazz, open your bags and let us examine the clover you have collected," instructed Mastis.

The two students reverently opened their bags and, as they did so, sparkling lights danced from within and a beam of light shot up to the sky. Mastis examined the contents of each bag. "An especially fine collection. You have both done very well. Now, take out one flower and place the blossom in your mouth."

Jazz did so without hesitation but Nick reached into his bag, removed one twinkling clover, and held it up in front of his face. He trusted Mastis; yet, at the same time, he was nervous about what the flower would do once it was inside his body.

"Have no fear, Nicholas," said Shema soothingly. "The clover will not hurt you."

Slowly and deliberately, Nick placed the sparkling flower onto his tongue and closed his mouth. He immediately wanted to laugh as he felt the flower pop and fizzle inside his mouth as it dissolved. In just a matter of moments, the ticklish sensation stopped and the flower was gone.

"You now have a magic power within you that can be called upon to make you invisible. Squeeze your eyes shut and draw on the power inside of you to pull in your light. When you open your eyes, you will be invisible to all around you," instructed Mastis.

Nick and Jazz did so and when they opened their eyes, neither could see the other. "Jazz? Where are you?" asked Nick as he reached out to where his horse had been standing just a moment before. With a gasp, he pulled his hand back.

He could feel his hand but he couldn't see it. He touched his body all over, feeling its form but unable to see any of it. The sensation reminded him of the hike his family had taken in a cave. Their guide had instructed them to turn out their lights. There, in the complete darkness, Nick had not been able to see any part of his body. He had touched his face and torso to be sure that all of his body parts were still there. That was the same sensation he was experiencing now except that this time everything else around him was still visible.

As he stood there with his arms folded across his chest and grasping his elbows with the opposite hand in an attempt to hold onto himself, he looked around. He could see Mastis looking toward him and Shema frolicking about in excitement. He could see his bag of clover where he had set it on the ground and Jazz's bag as well, but Jazz was completely invisible.

"How long does this last?" Nick asked and was shocked that his voice sounded as though it was echoing through a hollow chamber.

"The magic from one clover can last inside a unicorn's body for two days. I really don't know how long it will stay in your body, Nicholas, as we have never tried using it with a human before. Since your body is so much smaller than ours, I am inclined to think that it could last much longer," replied Mastis.

"That's comforting," said Nick with a chuckle. "So how do I become myself again?"

Shema jumped in with excitement, "You simply reverse the process by squeezing your eyes shut and letting your light out. When you open your eyes again, you will have returned to normal."

Nick and Jazz responded simultaneously and both reappeared.

Mastis curled his front legs and lowered himself to the grass. He pointed to the ground with his glowing horn to invite the others to join him.

"I must instruct you in the proper use of the invisible clover," he began once everyone was settled comfortably on the ground. "The clover will only work with those who have mastered the power to control the elements and to heal. That is why this was the last skill that I taught you. As you know, all of your powers will leave you if you do not use them for good and to serve others. The power to become invisible is useful for protection, and we unicorns use this power often when we go through the mist to help an animal. As I mentioned, the magic in one flower will last in a unicorn or horse for two days. Nicholas, we will have to test the results on you. In any case, you need to be prepared with extra flowers if you should go on a long journey. You can make other things invisible with you just by holding on to them. We often carry dying animals through the mist in an invisible state." At this point, Mastis stopped and let out a long sigh. Nick, who had been looking down at his bag of clover, looked up and found Mastis's eyes were studying him intently.

"Yes, Mastis, I am still committed to rescuing Bethany."

"You have no idea how hard and dangerous that will be."

"I don't care. Saving her is what I must do. I know that is my purpose for being here."

"And I will be with you," inserted Jazz.

"I would be eternally grateful if you could bring back my Bethany, eternally grateful, indeed," said Shema. "But I would never ask such a thing of you."

"Hasbadana will exercise all of his powers in an effort to turn you from the light. He will use every tool at his disposal. Resisting him will be very difficult. You also must realize that Shema and I cannot go with you."

"I know that. Jazz and I will use all of the power within us and all of the skills that you have taught us. We will succeed," responded Nick, though his words belied the anxiety he felt in his heart.

Jazz, sensing the doubts Nick was feeling, turned to him. "You have not been given the power of fear but of love."

"Just keep reminding me, my friend," said Nick with a nervous chuckle.

"I do not have the authority to give you permission to undertake such a treacherous journey. We will go to meet with the Council tomorrow and see if they will give you their blessing," Mastis explained as he slowly gathered his legs beneath him and stood up. "Until then," he said with a bow.

Light as a deer, the magnificent unicorn sprang out of the clearing.

Shema walked with them back to their cottage. "I want you to know that I love Bethany very much, very, very much," she said as they walked. "Unfortunately, her Earth life was so unhappy that she had no reservoir of love to fight off Hasbadana's influence. Healing her enough to pull her away from him will be difficult."

Nick reached over and stroked Shema's neck as they walked along. *Jazz,* he thought, *can we do this?* His feelings of confidence and the bravado he had expressed in the meadow were gone now.

We can do this…together, was the reply.

Mastis, along with Shema, came to gather his students just as the sun came up. With Nick riding Jazz, the four of them headed off to meet with the Council of the Twelve Ancients and the Lord Urijah.

As Mastis, Shema, Jazz, and Nick approached the beautifully carved cliff with its tall, colored spires, Nick noticed that the enormous golden doors were standing open as if awaiting their arrival. When the four companions entered the great hall, all of the hustling and bustling unicorns stopped in mid-stride and stared at them. A few whispered to one another, keeping their eyes glued to the little group. Nick looked up to see the dancing animals that represent the unicorn virtues. However, this time the animal carvings were not dancing. Each figure surrounding the dome was frozen in place, their eyes staring directly at him. The ceiling did not change colors nor send down bursts of stars to the floor. Instead, it glowed with a bright blue color. The difference in the atmosphere between this visit and the last was a bit unnerving. Obviously, everyone in the beautiful Council chambers was not only expecting them, but was also aware of why they had come.

Only the beautiful music that filled the air brought any comfort to Nick. He let its melody fill his soul and give him the strength he needed to continue forward and approach the great doors at the end of the hall. The two enormous chestnut unicorns that guarded the doors welcomed them with a nod, but not with a smile. Nick could not read the expressions on their faces. Was it suspicion or concern that they were reflecting? In any case, the centurions stepped aside without speaking and the beautiful doors opened.

Inside the room, the Lord of the kingdom of Celestia and his Council of Twelve Ancients were once again arranged in a semicircle. The colors that emanated from their bodies danced around the room. The sight was so beautiful that Nick felt a renewed sense of purpose and confidence. He slid off Jazz's back and bowed to the thirteen unicorns, all of whom stood silently watching him.

Urijah was the first to speak. "Welcome, Nicholas and Jazz. Helam informs me that your training is complete and that you and Jazz have learned your lessons well. I am so pleased.

Mastis, you should be congratulated on your excellent work with these two foals."

"Instructing them was a pleasure, Urijah. Thank you for the opportunity."

"Yes, well, who better suited?" Urijah responded with a warm smile. "Now, let us turn to the business at hand, shall we? The Council understands that you, Nicholas and Jazz, have come before us with a most unusual and, shall I say, dangerous proposal."

"Yes, my Lord," said Nick, surprising even himself with his audacity. "We have met the other human who was brought into Celestia. She had been sent by Hasbadana to spy on our training. Before we could help her, she disappeared. We assume she was taken back to the Dark Kingdom. Since Jazz is not yet a unicorn and I, obviously, will never be…" all of the Council members smiled at this, "we desire to go into the Dark Kingdom to rescue her from Hasbadana's control."

"You realize that she may not want to be rescued?" interjected Helam.

Shema immediately responded to Helam's query. "Oh, my Lord, I know Bethany. Yes, she is weak, she has been beaten down and abused, but she is filled with goodness. I know that if Nicholas and Jazz could reach her and give her the strength she needs, she would reject Hasbadana and return to me…us." Tears immediately filled Shema's eyes and quietly flowed down over her cheekbones.

"You feel sure of her character, Shema?" asked Urijah kindly, sensing her pain.

"Yes, Lord, I do. I do indeed," said Shema, turning back toward Urijah.

Urijah turned to look at Nick and Jazz once again. "Nicholas and Jazz, I am quite sure that you do not comprehend the danger you will be putting yourselves in by traveling to the Dark Kingdom. Hasbadana has tremendous powers of persuasion. He desires to take your light and use the power that lies within you for his own selfish purposes. He will attempt to enslave you and dominate you. Here in Celestia you have freedom. You may choose your course. In the Dark Kingdom, you would have no such freedom. He will dictate your every action, and those actions might not be for your own good or the good of others. You would eventually lose all of the light within you. Since you are already immortal, he does not have the power to kill you, only to destroy you."

These words made Nick shudder, but gaining strength by placing his hand on Jazz's neck, he spoke up. "Mastis has warned me about Hasbadana's power and his methods. I know that I am naive, but I believe that Jazz and I have enough love within us to withstand the dark one."

"And they will have my love for Bethany to take with them as well," added Shema.

Silence filled the Council chambers for several minutes. The Lord of the kingdom of Celestia looked at his Council members one by one, pausing at each to listen to their thoughts on the matter. Nick could tell that they were communicating and he wished that he had the power to hear what they were discussing. Almost at once, Mastis's thoughts entered Nick's head. *They are pleased with your power. They trust you.* Nick turned toward the dapple-gray unicorn and smiled.

"Nicholas and Jazz," said Urijah in a commanding yet kind voice, "one of the guiding tenets in Celesta is the biblical principle of agency. You have the freedom and power to make your own choices. You do not need our permission to go to the Dark Kingdom. However, we are pleased that you have chosen to come to us for our blessing before undertaking such a dangerous quest. We have decided to grant you our blessing. I, the Lord of Celestia, and my Council of the Twelve Ancients will send with you the power of love that is within us. We hope that this will sustain you."

At this, each of the twelve Council members, led by Helam, stepped up to Nick and Jazz. One by one they touched their glowing horns on Nick's right shoulder, then his left, then his forehead. They did the same for Jazz, touching first his right shoulder, then his left, and then they placed the tip of their horn on the double cowlick between his eyes. As each unicorn gave their blessing of love, Nick felt a warm, tingling sensation traverse through his body. Nick could feel the love within him swell until he thought he might burst.

When each of the Twelve Ancients returned to their places, Urijah came forward. He stopped for a moment before them. His eyes were filled with love as he looked down at them. He, too, touched their shoulders and forehead with his magnificent horn. He took a step back. "The love we have given you will make you more powerful than you would be on your own."

Nick and Jazz bowed before the great and wise unicorn. "Thank you," was all that the two could or needed to say. Shema was too overcome with emotion to say anything as she stood to the side of them and cried. Mastis stood still as well, his head held high and proud.

chapter 13

The Journey Begins

P reparations for the trip were quite easy. The only thing Jazz and Nick needed to take with them were their shoulder bags filled with the invisible clover. Mastis and Shema decided to accompany them to the edge of the Dark Kingdom.

With his confidence fully intact, Nick looked around his cottage. Warmth filled his heart as he looked around his little home and he hoped that he would be back to his comfortable down bed soon. He stepped out into the sun-filled clearing where Jazz, Mastis, and Shema were waiting for him.

"What direction are we going, Mastis?" Nick asked.

"We will accompany you northward to the point where the light meets the dark."

"What will we do then?"

"You will step into the dark," was Mastis' reply. With that, Mastis turned and led the way into the woods that surrounded Nick and Jazz's clearing. They traveled throughout the day in the opposite direction from the way they had traveled to visit the Council and Mt. Elisia. At some point, the meadows of flowers began to give way to fields and trees that were not quite so lush. The surrounding land looked more like the Earth that Nick had come from, still beautiful but not as bright and colorful. As he continued looking around, Nick started to see lots of animals. He noticed horses grazing in a lush, green pasture in the shade of a giant oak tree. The scene looked like the pastoral images depicted in paintings by George Stubbs. Nick was familiar with most, though not all, of the species of animals they came upon. "Are we still in Celestia?" he asked his guides.

"No, we left Celestia at the edge of that last meadow. We have entered the Animal Kingdom. This is where the animals come after their Earth life. You will notice that their behaviors are different than they would have been on Earth," said Mastis with a smile.

Nick looked around. Indeed, things were different here. At one point he noticed several lions grazing among a herd of oxen. Farther along he came upon some bear cubs curled up and sleeping with young lambs. After traveling for several hours, Nick noticed something unusual. "Why don't I see any dogs here?" asked Nick.

"Oh, that is true. There are very few dogs. You see, most of the dogs choose to go to the Human Kingdom. In fact, poodles were actually insulted at the mere suggestion that they stay in the Animal Kingdom," said Shema with a chuckle.

Nick smiled to himself as he thought of, Belle, the poodle who had been such an important part of his family until her death the year before his own death. Knowing that she was with the rest of his family was comforting. He took a moment to daydream about Belle playing with his little sisters, Lynn and Nancy. He smiled to himself as he thought of the time he had taken her to an off-leash dog park, and how he thought she would love to run and play with the other dogs. Belle had spent the entire time sitting next to him and the other people on the picnic bench, watching the dogs run around.

116

One kind woman had come up to her and asked, "Don't you want to play with the other dogs?" Belle had turned to examine her with a look of such disdain that the woman caught her breath and responded, "Oh, pardon me. I see that you are not a dog!"

With his thoughts coming back to where they were traveling, Nick said with a laugh, "No wonder there are so many cats here." Both of the unicorns, amused by Nick's joke, snorted and let out a chuckle-like whinny.

As they journeyed through the Animal Kingdom, they were constantly greeted by groups of animals. "Welcome, Mastis and friends," one said.

"It is such a pleasure to see you," joined in another.

"Shema! It has been far too long since I have seen you," said one enthusiastic giraffe, bringing his head down out of the highest tree limbs.

"Do you come here often, Mastis?" asked Jazz.

"Oh, yes. I have many friends here. I have brought many of them through the mist when it was their time."

At sunset, they were greeted by a group of beavers. "We have prepared a lovely hut for you to rest in for the night," they said as the group of now-weary travelers approached.

Mastis, Shema, Nick, and Jazz followed the beavers to an enormous mound of sticks and logs. On one side was an opening large enough for the unicorns to enter if they dipped their heads to the level of their withers. Inside the hut was straw for the three equines and a lovely mossy bed for Nick. The beavers stood without, obviously pleased with their creation, and awaited the response from their visitors.

"This was so kind of you," said Mastis.

"Yes, indeed. I have never seen such an inviting bed," added Shema.

Nick went over to each beaver and stroked the wiry hair on their heads. "Thank you so much, my friends."

Soon, animals of all types began bringing them food. Fruits, vegetables, breads, and cheeses of all types were placed in front of them. All four filled themselves until they felt their bodies renewed and restored. Lively conversation took place between Mastis, Shema, and their hosts. The animals were eager to share with their saviors what they had been doing since they last met. For some, the time since leaving Earth had been short, for others that event had been long ago. Joy and happiness filled all the tales they had to tell.

What a happy place this is, thought Nick.

Indeed it is, was Jazz's reply.

Suddenly, the happy chatter stopped and all of the animals turned their heads toward the side of the stick hut. Nick and Jazz turned to look at what had caught their attention. There, just stepping out of the shadow of the mound, was a beautiful dark bay horse. Jazz's head came up with a start and he stood up quickly. The horse continued moving toward him, walking with the elegance of a queen. The other animals parted to let her through until she was nose to nose with the Hanoverian.

"My son," she whispered. Jazz and his mother blew warm air into one another's nostrils and intertwined their necks in a horse's version of a hug.

"My son, I am so proud of you," said his mother quietly but with enthusiasm and excitement. Jazz had been weaned from his mother when he was a yearling and had only seen her briefly after that, but his love for her had never diminished. She had raised him with patience and kindness and had instilled those qualities in her son. The mare stepped back. "Let me look at you. What a handsome fellow you are! And to think you have been selected to become a unicorn," she said, her voice rising with exhilaration. "That is every mare's dream: to have a filly or colt of her own grow up to become a unicorn."

Jazz took the compliment with some degree of embarrassment, well aware that all eyes were on the two of them. "I wanted my Earth life to be a jewel in your crown, Mother," he said quietly.

"Come, let us visit somewhere that is a bit more private," she said with a smile at her animal friends, all of whom looked quickly away, aware that they were intruding on a sacred moment.

Nick watched Jazz and his mother leave the group and go off a short distance from the group. He felt a sudden, strong pang of homesickness for his own parents and sisters. Tears of both joy and sadness welled up in his eyes as he watched them. Even though he was a bit embarrassed to do so, he couldn't help but listen to the conversation through Jazz's thoughts. Jazz talked with his mother about his Earth life— his successful career as a Grand Prix Dressage horse; his kind owners, trainers, and riders; and about his retirement in the Rocky Mountains in a land called Colorado. He spoke of Nick and the bond that had formed between them. He also told her about the lightning and thunderstorm and their fall down the cliff, about Mastis' appearance, and Jazz's refusal to go behind the mist without Nick.

All this time, his mother listened with rapt attention. When he began telling her about Celestia and the land of the unicorns, tears of joy welled up in her eyes. When he told her about the mission they were on to go into the Dark Kingdom and save Bethany, a look of fear replaced the tears in her eyes.

"Did Urijah approve this mission?" she asked.

"Yes, and he gave us his blessing."

"He gave you his blessing? Then you will succeed," was her only reply.

That night, the dreams returned. Nick could see Bethany in a cold, damp, stone room. She was shivering from both the temperature and fear. She was alone. There was no sound other than her labored breathing. Nick forced himself awake. He sat up and looked over to see Jazz and both of the unicorns looking at him from their beds.

"Another dream about Bethany," stated Jazz. "She is in urgent need of our help."

"Yes," said Nick as an involuntary shiver went through his body.

Morning came in the Animal Kingdom and the four travelers bid their hosts farewell and continued on their journey. They started traveling on a narrow trail that curved its way downhill and through trees and shrubs. By the end of the morning, they found themselves at the edge of a wide and wild river.

"Nicholas and Jazz, will you create a boat for us? If we ride down the river we can reach the Dark Kingdom before nightfall and save our energy at the same time," said Mastis.

Nick and Jazz set to work immediately. They had become adept at commanding the elements and before long they had turned several trees into a sturdy, sea-worthy, flat-bottomed boat. As a creative touch, Nick added the bust of a unicorn on the bow; the sculpture's horn pointed forward and the front legs curled up below the chest as though the unicorn were leaping out of the boat and over the waves.

Nick climbed on top of Jazz and they gently stepped into the boat, followed by Shema and Mastis. They all turned and faced down stream. Jazz commanded the waters to carry them to the center of the river and to smooth their path. The waters complied and their little boat began its journey down the river.

The trip was going smoothly. They all began chattering light-heartedly as they sailed along. River animals from turtles to crocodiles swam along beside them for a time, sharing in their conversation. Nick shared a story of becoming terribly seasick while sailing on a catamaran around St. Maarten in the Caribbean. He had done quite well while sailing up the west side of the island, but once they had rounded the northern tip of the island and entered the waters of the Atlantic he had become uncontrollably nauseated. Sailing had not been a pleasant experience!

Jazz had not spent any time on water but had flown over the ocean in an airplane when he was being shipped to the United States from Germany. Mastis had been swimming in the ocean off the coast of the place called California. With each tale, they moved closer and closer to the Dark Kingdom. No one wanted to talk about that at the moment.

After sailing along swiftly but smoothly for several hours, Nick noticed that the river was growing much narrower and beginning to move much faster. Ahead of them, he heard a roaring sound that continued to grow louder and louder. After sailing around a bend in the river, Nick saw what was making the noise. Ahead of them, the river dropped completely out of sight. Nick suddenly had the sick feeling that he was about to find out what going over Niagara Falls in a barrel must be like.

"Mastis, what do we do?" asked Nick in a near panic.

"Command the elements. They will obey," was Mastis' calm reply.

Nick slid off Jazz's back and stepped to the front of the boat. He looped one arm around his unicorn carving and looked ahead at the water, watching the river disappear from sight. He did not know how high the cliff or long the fall was, but one thing he did know was that he needed to create a plan quickly. An image filled his mind; what made him think of it, he did not know, but he suddenly remembered once seeing an elevator on the outside of a hotel in New York City. He had been fascinated as he had watched the cubical carry its cargo of hotel guests up and down the outside of the building, stopping at selected floors while people disembarked. At that moment he knew just what to do.

"River, I command you to form a ledge of water to carry us down the face of the waterfall without letting us fall forward."

With some trepidation, Nick watched the front of the boat where he stood sail to the top of the falls. He looked straight ahead as the boat headed out over the edge and seemed to hang in midair. The water flowed beneath the boat and held the vessel there for a moment. Slowly, Nick became aware that they were moving down. He gathered the courage to look below the boat and saw that the waterfall was incredibly long, but they were moving slowly down the face of the falls in a perfectly perpendicular position as a shelf of water, holding them securely, gently lowered them down the falls.

When they reached the bottom of the falls, the river pushed them forward as though the water possessed hands. With this assistance, they continued on their journey. The river began flowing through a deep canyon. High cliffs surrounded them on both sides. Shadows darkened the water ahead of them. Nick looked at the dark water and could not escape the feeling of foreboding that filled his heart.

Once they sailed past the canyon walls, the river made a sharp turn to the south. Mastis commanded the water to carry them to the far shore. "Here we will disembark and continue our journey to the Dark Kingdom on foot," he said.

Nick hopped onto Jazz's back and the two unicorns and the horse stepped out of the boat onto the shore and continued north. The ground had become much more barren and much rockier, reminding Nick of Rocky Mountain National Park above the timberline. All was still and quiet around them and none of the friends spoke. Each was lost in thought.

Shortly before the sun set, Mastis broke the silence. "There is the Dark Kingdom."

They all stopped and looked forward. Not far ahead, was the strangest sight Nick had ever seen. The light simply stopped, like a child's painting of the sky depicted only as a line of blue. Beyond, there was a wall of darkness. From a distance the wall appeared to be solid.

Jazz was the first to step forward. Mastis and Shema followed a stride behind. When they arrived at the place where the light meets the dark, they all stopped once again. Nick and Jazz turned to look at their saviors.

"We must leave you now, my foals. You have learned your lessons well. You have been blessed with an endowment of tremendous love by the Council. You will succeed. We shall eagerly await your return to the light," said Mastis gently.

Shema just stood and cried.

Without saying a word, Jazz turned and, with Nick on his back, stepped into the dark.

⇥ chapter 14 ⇤
The Dark Kingdom

The moment Jazz and Nick entered the Dark Kingdom, everything around them was different. They stopped and examined this strange new environment in an attempt to make sense of all that they were seeing and feeling. It took Nick's mind a few minutes to put together all of the elements of their surroundings. No sunlight was able to penetrate the darkness. Nick located the sun in the sky, but it appeared that he was looking at it through a layer of dense smoke, the way people in Washington and Oregon had described the sun after the eruption of Mount St. Helens in 1981. As a result, no shadows were cast by the sun which seemed to be constantly changing its orientation. The sky was many shades of gray. The air was cold. A strong wind blew from all directions at once. The ground was barren and colorless. The trees, as Nick had seen in one of his dreams, were void of leaves and stood apart from one another as though afraid to touch. All of this was unnerving enough, but the most intimidating characteristic was the silence. The silence that permeated the darkness made Nick's ears hurt and he covered them with his hands. Both Nick and Jazz were afraid to turn their heads and look back at the Animal Kingdom for fear they would lose their resolve and not continue on.

There was one source of light for Nick and Jazz: the light emanating from their bodies. The light from within them radiated outward, lighting their surroundings for about five feet in all directions.

Nick spoke first. "Well, I guess we had better get this over with," he said, stroking Jazz's strong neck.

"Which way do we go?"

Nick took a deep breath. "Let me listen."

He closed his eyes against the darkness and sent his mind through the silence. Gradually, he became aware of Bethany's thoughts. It wasn't so much that he could hear words, but rather that he could feel her spirit. He clung to this awareness as he sent Jazz forward with a squeeze of his legs. As Jazz began galloping over the ground with incredible speed, Nick guided him in the direction he should go. When they took a wrong turn, the force from Bethany's spirit became weaker. Each time they veered out of alignment, Nick directed Jazz to change course, much like dialing a radio to pick up a signal.

The farther they traveled, the darker their surroundings became until it seemed that they were journeying during a moonless night. Suddenly, Jazz's head came up and his ears turned to the side. Nick also heard a rustling sound break the silence and looked in the same direction. Jazz kept moving at his same astonishing speed even though neither Nick nor Jazz could see what had made the sound.

"What was that?" asked Nick, trying to control the nervousness he felt.

"I don't know," Jazz responded.

The rustling sound happened again and again. Something was moving along beside them. Whatever was out there was keeping pace with them. Yet they could not see anything. "We have company," said the gelding, never missing a stride or slowing down. Nick looked to the side and strained his eyes as he peered into the darkness. Though he couldn't see anything, he could hear it. Something was indeed running beside them.

As suddenly as the sound appeared, it disappeared and Nick and Jazz were left with the overwhelming silence once again. *I guess we lost them,* thought Nick.

Somehow I don't think so. This is their territory, responded Jazz in his thoughts.

Nick went back to concentrating on listening for Bethany's thoughts and a stab of panic filled his heart. "Stop, Jazz! I've lost her."

Jazz stopped immediately and began walking in a slow circle. After nearly completing an entire circle, Nick felt Bethany's presence again. "This way," he said pointing in the direction they were now facing. Jazz leaped forward, almost unseating his passenger, and sped off in the direction Nick pointed.

Soon they heard another rustling sound, but this time it was on both sides of them. *We have company again,* thought Nick to his horse.

I know. Let them come along if they want; I don't care, responded Jazz as he lengthened his strides and began covering a seemingly impossible amount of ground with each stroke of his long legs.

Through the darkness they traveled. Nick tried to ignore the rustling sounds around them as he focused on Bethany. After a while, these visitors also left them alone, but more of their unseen escorts joined them farther ahead as though they were a relay team. None of their company showed themselves or tried to stop them, however, so Nick and Jazz continued on unmolested. Again, without warning, the sound of their company's footsteps abruptly stopped.

Without warning, Jazz's strides came nearly to a stop and Nick almost fell off. Jazz lifted both front legs up and lunged forward with his powerful hind quarters.

"What's the matter? What is it?" shouted Nick, surprising himself that his voice came out so loudly.

"I've run into some thick mud which keeps trying to grab my legs and pull me down," said Jazz in a panic. He reared up and bound forward again. As he lifted his front feet, Nick could hear a loud sucking sound. Nick held on tightly to a chunk of Jazz's mane in an attempt to keep from sliding off the gelding's back.

"This isn't mud, this is quicksand! Can you carry us out of here?" asked Nick, fear rising in his voice.

"I don't know which way to go. I can't see far enough ahead."

Gaining some composure, Nick said, "We must use our powers."

"Yes, quickly! I'm becoming exhausted."

While Jazz continued to rear up and lunge forward, Nick called forth the power within him. "Sand, I command you to let go of Jazz's legs and form a firm bridge that we may travel upon."

With slurping and gurgling sounds, the ground beneath them began solidifying. The viscous sand became hard and Jazz was able to scramble on top. He stood with his head and neck low as he gasped for breath. Nick stroked his neck and patiently waited while his horse rested. Finally, Jazz's head came up and off they went.

Nick's connection to Bethany's spirit was growing stronger and stronger and it was now quite easy to stay on course. After a long and exhausting journey, Nick sensed that they were close. Suddenly, something inside of him told him to stop. Jazz could hear his thoughts and stopped abruptly.

From the light cast by their bodies, they could see that they had stopped right at the rim of a deep, dark canyon. Nick's and Jazz's hearts beat loudly as the realization of the danger they had been in bore down on them.

Nick slid off Jazz's back and stepped up beside the gelding's head. Together they looked down. They could not see the bottom of the cliff upon which they stood. Darkness was all that greeted them.

"That was a close one, Jazz," said Nick aloud and, even though he had tried to whisper, he was again surprised at the volume of his voice.

"Indeed, it was. Where do we go from here?" asked Jazz.

Nick lifted his head and looked straight ahead into the darkness. "She is out there."

"But how do we reach her?"

"I don't know where this goes. We need to be able to see ahead of us," responded Nick with frustration in his voice.

"I know what to do," said Jazz with conviction. Nick turned to look at him and saw him close his eyes. Nick jumped back in surprise as a ball of light shot forth from Jazz's forehead. Like a Fourth of July firework, the ball of light traveled through the sky and exploded high in the air, casting a bright light all around them.

"Wow, Jazz! That was awesome," exclaimed Nick. But their enthusiasm was short-lived.

Nick and Jazz gasped as they looked at the scene before them. They stood at the edge of a circular crater. The edges of the crater went straight down for hundreds of feet. In the center of the crater was a tall, stone pedestal. Built on top of the pedestal was a brick-and-stone building. Nick felt his heart drop to his stomach as he realized that Bethany was in that structure. Jazz must have known the same thing.

"How will we reach her?" asked Nick as he looked around at the barren ground.

"There must be a way. They took her to that tower somehow, didn't they?" responded Jazz.

"Let's find it then," said Nick as he hopped back on Jazz's back. They started searching the perimeter of the crater, hoping the light from the glowing orb that Jazz had created would last long enough to find an access to the center tower.

They had traveled halfway around the circular crater's edge when they found what they were searching for. There was a jagged chasm cut into the edge of the cliff. Within this rift, steps wound down into the darkness. Nick slid off Jazz and started down the stairway. Jazz paused for a moment before starting down behind his trusted partner.

Down into the dark crater the stairs wound and Nick and Jazz followed them step by step. Once they had descended nearly a hundred feet, the stairway opened into the crater itself and connected to an arched bridge that reached across to the pedestal. Looking down, they were still unable to see the bottom of the crater.

"Don't you think it's weird that we haven't seen any of the dark unicorns yet?" asked Nick as the two of them looked across at the towering structure that served as Bethany's jail. "I can't believe that they don't know we're here."

"Oh, I am quite sure that they do know we are here," replied Jazz. "Something was following us. Perhaps this is a trap and they want us to go in there."

"Perhaps it is. However, we have no choice if we are going to save Bethany," said Nick. Mustering all the power of the love within him, he stepped onto the archway.

⟶ chapter 15 ⟵

Bethany

ick and Jazz walked slowly across the arched bridge connecting the cliff walls to the towering pedestal. Nick became aware, once again, of the deafening silence. The only thing he could hear were the clip-clopping sounds of Jazz's four hooves as they stepped along the stone bridge. At one point, Nick looked over the side into the darkness beneath. He still could not see the bottom of the crater.

Just as they reached the far side, Jazz's glowing sphere that had given them light all this time diminished then went out completely. Only the glowing radiance from their bodies provided them any light. They entered an open doorway in the side of the column. The light radiating from their bodies revealed another staircase, this one spiraling up through the middle of the tower. Nick turned and looked sympathetically at Jazz. Stairs are easy for a biped to negotiate, but a horse must control the position of four feet so stairs are a difficult challenge for them. Jazz snorted in apparent disgust and gave Nick a nudge forward with his big head. Nick stumbled from the push but caught himself just in time to negotiate the first step. Up the staircase he went with Jazz following close behind.

Anyone who has climbed the historic 125-foot Astor Column in Astoria, Oregon, knows what they were going through. Each step was not only steep but part of a long spiral staircase. Nick became winded quickly and perspiration dripped into his eyes. He had to stop and rest frequently. Even his immortal body was tired, the muscles complained and the lungs ached. With utmost concentration, he was able to finish the trek and reach the top where a door stood ajar.

Nick paused at the door and Jazz stopped behind him.

Is she inside? thought Jazz.

Yes, I'm sure of it. I can feel her presence strongly.

Is she alone?

Nick paused and listened carefully, trying to separate his thoughts from Jazz's and Bethany's to see if there was anyone or anything else present. *I think so. I can't feel anyone else. Shall we enter?*

That's what we came for, replied Jazz.

Nick started to step through the doorway, but a strong impression filled his mind and he stopped with his foot in midair. Setting his foot down quietly, he asked Jazz,

Doesn't it seem like this has been too easy? Why hasn't Hasbadana tried to stop us? Surely he knows we are in the Dark Kingdom.

Yes, he knows. I have no doubt about that. I do not understand his motives. Let us proceed with our mission and deal with what comes.

I feel that now would be the time to use our invisible clover. I don't think we need to become invisible but we should at least have their magic inside of us so we can become invisible if need be, suggested Nick in his thoughts.

That is a wise idea. The clover may come in handy, replied Jazz and he turned his head around to his shoulder. With his nimble lips, he opened his bag and took out one clover. Nick reached to his side and slid his hand into the bag. He grasped one flower, took it out of the bag and marveled at the twinkling light at the end of the stem. He placed the flower head in his mouth. The sweetness of it filled his mouth as it dissolved. He looked over at Jazz. *Are you ready?* The gelding nodded his head, sending his forelock bouncing over his eyes. *Perhaps you should speak to her. Remember, she trusted you more than me,* said Nick

That is another wise suggestion, responded Jazz. So, with a quiet and loving voice Jazz spoke. "Bethany, are you in there? It is I, Jazz, the horse that you met in Celestia. I am here with my friend, Nicholas. May we come in?"

At once, there was a response, but it was no more than a low groan. Nick and Jazz entered the room, bringing their light with them. The room was made of rock. The walls were made of jagged stones, fitted together like a jigsaw puzzle. The floor was only slightly smoother. A few slits in the walls allowed cold air and wind to enter. There was no source of light, only cold, silent darkness.

When Nick saw Bethany he gasped. There, in the corner of the small, square room was her body, resembling a crumpled up newspaper or a pile of rubbish. A quiet groan crossed the room to greet them. Nick could feel anger well up inside of him. With a conscious effort, he pushed the anger away and replaced the feeling with love. *Love is the source of my power,* he reminded himself.

Nick ran to her and knelt beside her. He tenderly lifted her shoulders and head and set them on his lap. He gently brushed her tangled hair away from her face. The light radiating from Nick's hand fell on Bethany's face and she squeezed her eyes tightly shut and covered her face with her hands. Her hands were so thin they were no more than bones covered with parchment-like skin. Her fingernails were short and dirty.

Nick stroked her forehead and dirty hair as he cradled her on his lap. Jazz stood over them, rubbing his muzzle along her emaciated body.

The odor in the room and emitting from Bethany's body was so unpleasant that Nick felt nauseated. He looked around the dimly lit room and commanded the foul smell to depart. Instantly, the odor was replaced by a fresh smell like a field right after a spring rain. Jazz used his powers to clean Bethany's body and cover her with a clean garment. This small effort seemed to have an instant effect upon Bethany and she dropped her hands from her face and squinted at her visitors.

A warm and beautiful smile filled her face and reached her eyes. For the first time, Nick could see a twinkling in what had been a dark void. "You came. I never thought you would, but here you are." Tears flowed down her cheeks and she turned and buried her face in Nick's chest.

"Bethany," said Nick. "We have come to take you away from here. We have come to take you back to Celestia with us."

She lifted her head and looked into his eyes. Once again, Nick could see the tiniest twinkle of light in her eyes. "Oh no, I can never leave here. Hasbadana won't allow it and I am not worthy to go to Celestia. But it doesn't matter. I am content just knowing that you cared enough to come here. That knowledge will bring me the comfort that I need."

"No, Bethany," interjected Jazz. "You cannot stay here. Hasbadana will destroy you. You must come with us. We will help you. We will heal you. All of Celestia is awaiting your return. Shema, I mean Lady, is awaiting your return."

At the name of her beloved horse, Bethany turned and looked up at Jazz. "Lady? You know Lady?" she said, evidently forgetting their first conversation in Nick and Jazz's cottage.

"Oh yes. We know her by her new name of Shema. She is one of the unicorns who took care of us. She loves you and wants you to come back," replied Jazz while gently stroking her cheek with his muzzle. With each stroke, he sent into her all the power of love within him. With each stroke, Bethany, though not even aware of what was happening, was being healed little by little.

"But Hasbadana said she didn't want me, didn't love me," said Bethany weakly.

"He is the father of lies," said Nick, echoing the same words Jazz had used during their first meeting with Bethany. "Nothing he has told you is the truth. I have heard what he says. You mustn't believe him. You are not unlovable. You are of infinite worth. You were born to be good and kind and to be loved. If you will come with us, we will help you become the kind of person you were meant to be," said Nick, all the while stroking her head and sending his healing powers into her.

"How can this be? No one has ever loved me."

"It is true that you have been badly injured by those who should have cared for you and given you love, but that cannot take away the love that is innately yours nor the love that was given to you by the few others in your life who took the time to care. And Shema. Don't forget that Shema gave her life trying to be with you. She refused to come to Celestia without you. There is no greater love than to give of your life for someone else," said Nick, talking quicker and quicker as he stroked her head. He could feel her fragile, ice-cold body become ever so slightly warmer. He could see the glimmer of light growing in her eyes through the tears. Surely the love they had been blessed with by the Council of the Ancients was giving the two rescuers power beyond their own. This gave him a tremendous amount of encouragement.

Jazz's head came up with a start and his ears pinned back against his head. He let out a loud snort as he whirled toward the door.

There, just inside the room, stood Hasbadana and his two Clydesdale companions. These were the same Clydesdales that had brought Bethany to this prison. Nick recognized them immediately from Bethany's dreams. All three unicorns were large and angular. They radiated a coldness that accompanied the darkness they brought with them. Their eyes reflected the light from Nick and Jazz like pieces of black obsidian.

"Well, if it isn't the light communing with the dark," said Hasbadana with a sardonic smile. Turning to his companions he added, "Isn't that a touching portrait? Doesn't it make your heart pulsate a little faster within you?"

The two Clydesdales dutifully laughed at their leader's joke.

Abruptly, Hasbadana ceased his laughter. "Stop laughing!" he said, suddenly serious. "Is that any way to greet our long-awaited guests?" The two unicorns beside him became instantly silent and turned back toward Nick, Jazz, and Bethany.

With the graciousness of a python, Hasbadana lowered his voice. "My dear, dear Nicholas and his loyal steed, Jazz. Welcome to my kingdom. I trust that your journey here was pleasant and without incident? Hmm?"

Nick and Jazz said nothing. Nick continued to press his hands against Bethany and send his healing love into her, knowing instinctively that he had little time left to do so. Jazz stood between them, glaring at Hasbadana.

"Oh, I see. My brothers and sisters in Celestia poisoned you against me," saying the word "Celestia" as though it had a foul taste. "One really must learn not to be so gullible. The most intelligent of us all learn to study things out in our own minds before coming to any conclusions. I trust you are willing to be taught the truth of all things?"

"We need nothing from you. We have come only to retrieve Bethany and return her to Celestia, where she belongs," replied Jazz, never taking his eyes off Hasbadana.

A deep laugh erupted from Hasbadana's throat. His two cohorts, after looking at him for permission, joined in the laughter. They stopped as soon as Hasbadana did.

Turning his attention to Nick, "Oh, how vain the imaginations of the human heart." he said, keeping his voice paternal. "My boy, my boy, you think you know what is best for her. Yet what do you really comprehend of immortality? You think you have been endowed with great power. You know nothing of power!" He stepped forward and Jazz threw up his head, pinned his ears back and bared his teeth. Hasbadana's bodyguards responded in kind.

Hasbadana walked back and forth in front of them. "Patience, my friends. There is no reason to threaten our guests." Turning to Jazz he added, "We have come in peace. In point of fact, we have come as your benefactors." Turning his attention back to Nick, he continued, "Nicholas, listen to me. I can offer you far greater power than your underdeveloped mind can as yet comprehend. Come join me in my kingdom and participate in my greatness. Through the powers that I possess and the instincts that you have inherited by virtue of your humanhood, we can accomplish a great work. I will make you my trusted assistant. You will be by my side as we take our rightful place as the rulers of Earth." The evil unicorn's voice rose in volume and increased in tempo. He took his eyes off Nick and stared ahead of him at his own vision of the future. "No longer will animals be subject to the evil whims of mankind! We will band together and overpower the human race and the glory will be mine!"

Regaining his composure, he lowered his voice and looked back at Nick. "I had hoped that Bethany might be of assistance to me, but she has proven to be utterly worthless," he said, spitting out the last word. "But you, you Nicholas, have far greater potential. You have the ability to be instructed in the true order of things. You have learned your lessons well from the…shall I say, 'lower class of unicorns.' They are rudimentary tools to be sure, but they can help you to arrive at the place that I need you to be. You can help me understand the human mind. You can help me find their vulnerable places, their weaknesses." He continued pacing back and forth, staring intently at Nick.

All the while, Nick refused to look at him and focused only on infusing Bethany with love. Her body, though tense in response to Hasbadana's presence, continued to become warmer. A quiet, subtle light began to radiate from her skin.

Nicholas, keep concentrating on your work with Bethany. Do not listen to Hasbadana. He is only trying to distract you and win you over, thought Jazz.

Hasbadana continued. "Nicholas, if you will help me, I will make you ruler over the entire human race on Earth. I, of course, will take my rightful place as ruler of the Animal Kingdom. But you, you will be second only to me in your power and glory. All mankind will bow to you. Your every wish will be their command. Think of the possibilities," he said, his voice rising. "No human, with all their selfish desires and petty weaknesses, will have any power over you."

Hasbadana paused for a moment. Nick could hear him breathing heavily. For just a moment, Nick's thoughts turned to Hasbadana's words. The thought flashed through his mind, *Yes, I could use my power to bring great happiness to the world. I could help each person reach true joy by overcoming selfishness and…*

Stop! Focus only on Bethany. Jazz's thoughts entered his brain with great force. Nick shook his head to help him gain control of his thoughts once more.

"What say you, Nicholas? Will you join me and be my valued assistant as we help the poor, downtrodden animals of the Earth rise up to fulfill their destiny? They will sing your praises for all eternity even as they bow down before us," he said as his voice rose to a crescendo.

For a moment, Nick closed his eyes. He took a deep breath. When he opened his eyes, all of the equines were looking at him, awaiting his response. Jazz wasn't breathing as he focused his power, no longer on Bethany, but on Nick.

"Get thee behind me, Hasbadana! I will have none of your evil designs," he nearly shouted as he scooped up Bethany in his arms. He stood with his back to the three dark creatures. Turning just his head, and looking over his shoulder, he calmly yet boldly said, "We will be leaving now."

An evil laugh erupted once again from Hasbadana. His companions imitated him, stopping immediately when he resumed speaking. "You think it will be that easy? You think you can come into my kingdom and just take what belongs to me?"

"Bethany does not belong here nor does she belong to you," said Nick, surprising even himself with the calmness of his response.

"Oh, yes she does," roared Hasbadana. "She is filled with darkness and is unworthy to go to Celestia."

"No, you are wrong. She is full of light." With that, Nick turned around to reveal Bethany's softly glowing body. A weak smile formed on her face as she displayed enough courage to look into Hasbadana's fierce, cold eyes.

"You will spend the vast expanse of eternity, contemplating the darkest abyss," cursed Hasbadana loudly and the tower shook from the force of his anger. Suddenly, a ring of fire erupted around Nick, Bethany, and Jazz. The flames were so tall they lapped the ceiling, trapping them in a cage of fire.

Nick, realizing at once the natural fear horses have of fire, sent his thoughts to his companion: *There is no power in fear, only in love.*

Jazz stepped over closer to them. *Mount up on my back,* he commanded as he folded his front legs and lowered himself onto his knees. Nick set Bethany down just long enough to climb onto Jazz's slopping back then reached down and pulled her up in front of him. He marveled at how light she was. Sensing her weakness and feeling her tremble, he wrapped his arms tightly around her.

We must become invisible, Nick communicated to Jazz. Immediately, both Nick and Jazz squeezed their eyes shut and pulled their light inward. Because Nick was encircling Bethany with his arms, she, too, became invisible with them.

The heat from the flames was intense. Through the pulsating fingers of fire, Nick could see Hasbadana rearing and stomping. The two Clydesdale guards seemed to be frozen in place from their fear.

Nick quickly formed a plan. He realized that he had the power to command the flames to do his bidding. He decided that it would be wise to keep the ring of fire burning as a distraction. Jazz absorbed Nick's thoughts immediately. Jazz turned to the side and commanded the flames to refrain from touching them as they passed through. He confidently stepped forward. The red, orange, and yellow flames, the only color they had yet seen in the Dark Kingdom, rose up on either side of them, snapping and curling, but not touching them.

Once past the ring of fire, Jazz stealthily carried his precious cargo behind Hasbadana and his two guards, his hooves barely touching the stone floor, and silently exited the room through the stone doorway.

When they were safely away from the flames and the heat, Nick turned. "Rocks, I command you to enclose the room and fill in the doorway behind us." With a loud rumble, the entire tower shook and the rocks tumbled and rolled into place, sealing off the room that had been Bethany's prison. Loud squeals and screams could be heard from behind the stone blockade.

With all the speed and agility in him, Jazz charged down the winding staircase, leaving the sounds, flames, and heat behind them. They realized that the stone prison they had created would merely delay Hasbadana. Once Hasbadana became aware that they were gone, he would surely burst through the stone barrier they had created. Nick and Jazz needed to take advantage of every second they had. Nick struggled to keep his balance while holding tightly to Bethany as Jazz bounded down the spiral staircase. The tower began shaking even more violently and Nick and Jazz could still hear the shrieks of the three dark unicorns as they kicked at the stone-covered entrance. Pieces of rock began tumbling down the staircase after them.

Jazz struggled to keep his balance on the slippery, shaking stone steps. In their invisible state, their bodies did not radiate light so Jazz had to feel his way down each step as best he could. They had worked their way nearly halfway down when the tower gave a violent jolt and a barrage of boulders bounced down the stairway. Jazz stumbled as the loose stones rolled under his feet and legs. His hooves slid to one side, throwing his body against the wall. Nick cried out in pain as his leg was pinned against the rough side of the tower. He felt the rough stone tear through the fabric of his pants and into the skin and muscle of his leg. Even with the intense pain, he managed to keep a tight hold on Bethany. Jazz scrambled to his feet and stood upright again. "Are you both alright?" asked Jazz, panic evident in his voice.

"Yes, just keep going. We'll hold on," replied Nick between clenched teeth. He forced himself to concentrate on keeping himself securely on Jazz's back and steadying her weak body. He would simply have to ignore the pain shooting up his leg.

They reached the base of the tower and stepped onto the arched bridge just as a contingent of a dozen dark unicorns began galloping across the span from the far side. Jazz stepped to the side of the bridge and pressed his body against the wall of the tower. They waited silently in a cloak of invisibility while the unicorns began rushing over the bridge and through the tower's doorway. Four had charged into the tower before the fifth one stopped in his tracks. The unicorn soldier's head came up, his ears pinned back against his head, and his nostrils flared, pulsing slowly in and out. He slowly turned his head and stared directly toward them. He squinted in an attempt to see what could not be seen; his body quivered. Jazz pushed his body tighter against the wall; all three held their breath in an attempt at complete silence.

"Shazba, start moving," commanded a unicorn behind him.

With deliberate steps, the unicorn named Shazba stepped forward and into the tower entrance. The remaining unicorns rushed in and began their ascent of the curving staircase. Just as silently, though none of them could have heard him through the din of noise coming from the shaking tower and tumbling rocks, Jazz galloped across the bridge and began climbing the stairs that led to the rim of the crater.

Behind them, the dark unicorn named Shazba stepped out of the tower entrance and looked in all directions. He slowly stepped away from the tower and onto the arched bridge, his ears twitching in all directions, snorting to himself. Step by cautious step, he walked across the bridge.

⤙ chapter 16 ⤚

Escape

J ust as Jazz reached the fourth or fifth step, Nick yelled over the sound of the tumbling rocks, "Stop, Jazz!" Jazz stopped immediately and the two turned to look at the shaking, rumbling tower in the center of the crater lit from within by the glow of the flames.

"I have an idea," said Nick. He turned his attention to the arched bridge. Though exhausted from the power he had been exerting to heal Bethany, and the weakness he felt from the pain in his leg, he called upon the resources of love he had been given through the Council's blessing. "Bridge, I command you to fall into the darkest abyss," Nick commanded, echoing Hasbadana's curse.

Jazz turned his head and with a smile in his voice said, "So, I see you have learned the art of turning a phrase from our host."

"Yes, I guess we can even learn something from him," said Nick, weakly. They turned their attention back to climbing up the steps that lined the side of the crater. Neither one of them saw the body of a dark unicorn leap to the safety of the cliff ledge just as the bridge collapsed into the crater.

As the steps wove along the cliff wall and in and out of crevasses, Nick and Jazz caught glimpses of the burning tower. Flames reached high into the air. The heat from the fire and molten stone was intense at times. The noise created by the crashing boulders was in stark contrast to the silence that had accompanied their arrival. The flames created long and irregular shadows on the side of the crater, casting light on a stone face that may never have been illuminated before.

Just as they reached the top of the crater, they turned to look at the burning spectacle one last time. As if it had been waiting for an audience, the tower started collapsing from the top, crushing down upon itself one layer at a time. The noise was deafening. Dust and particles of sand filled the air, making it almost impossible to see through the thick smoke.

Nick gasped and gripped Jazz's mane tightly. He could not believe what his eyes were telling him. Rising up out of the smoke, flames and rubble, a massive dark shape appeared. As though he were rising on wings, Hasbadana, his eyes glowing red from the reflection of the flames and his body glistening black, leaped from the top of the collapsing structure. His powerful and significantly enlarged body carried him to the far side of the crater rim, opposite from where Jazz stood with Nick and Bethany on his back. As soon as the monster safely placed all four feet on the solid edge of the crater, he turned and stared toward them across the dark void through the smoke and dust. Even though Nick, Jazz, and Bethany were still under the power of the invisible clover, and Hasbadana could not see them, the intensity of his stare told them he was clearly aware of their presence. Suddenly, he rose up on his back legs, his enormous, angular body standing high in the air, his front legs thrashing through the billowing smoke, his head thrown back. An ear-splitting scream-like whinny reached them from across the crater, the threat clearly communicated.

A booming voice traveled across the abyss. "Nicholas, this will not be the last occasion that we will meet. I have offered you greatness and you have chosen to deny me. This will not be forgiven. You shall yet serve me. You shall yet crawl at my feet!" The evil unicorn whirled and disappeared into the darkness.

Nick cringed at the threat. Facing and standing up to evil was new to Nick and he felt especially small and inadequate. While keeping his grip on Jazz's mane and his arms around Bethany, he had a sudden thought. *I wonder what happened to Hasbadana's guards.*

"They must not have been strong enough to escape, but since they are immortal they have been cursed to spend eternity broken and buried deep in the bottom of the crater," said Jazz as he gazed over the edge of the cliff. A shudder went through Jazz's body and was reflected by Nick as they thought of the fate of the dark unicorns, a fate that was the result of their loyalty to Hasbadana.

When they turned away, their feelings were a mixture of relief for their own escape and a surprising amount of sadness and compassion for the fate of the unicorns. Both were thinking of how easily they could have been Hasbadana's victims. Of how, just earlier that day, Bethany had been under the control of the evil one. Of how Hasbadana took all his followers had to give but did not stand by his disciples when they were in trouble. *Hasbadana's power is selfishness, not love,* thought Nick, sharing his thoughts with Jazz.

He takes power from others and abandons them when they are of no further use to him. We must always remember the lesson we have learned today, responded Jazz.

Let's leave this horrible place, thought Nick.

Yes, I desire nothing more, but which way do we go?

Nick looked around them. They had traveled a long way around the edge of the crater, searching for the access to the tower. Would they recognize any landmarks that would tell them which way to go? Nick looked up at the sun. With its orientation constantly changing and its refusal to send light and warmth into the Dark Kingdom, the sun was of no help. He squeezed his eyes shut and sent out his light, attempting to return to visibility. But he was on top of Jazz and under the influence of his magic.

"Jazz, make yourself visible, I think we better save our strength until we need it." Jazz immediately closed his eyes and all three became visible again.

Suddenly, the light from their bodies created an astonishing result. There, in the rocky soil ahead of them, clearly visible in the surrounding darkness were Jazz's hoofprints, glowing as if made with reflective paint. They stepped forward onto the now visible path. As they walked forward, sending their light ahead of them, hoofprint after hoofprint lit up, clearly marking the way they had come.

Bethany, who had been silent all of this time from her perch in front of Nick, let out a sigh and a weak whimper. "He will never let us escape. He will come after us, I know he will." Silent tears rolled down her cheeks.

"He has no power over us unless we give it to him, Bethany. We will be alright," replied Jazz gently. The big, dark bay gelding broke into a gallop and began covering ground with strides much longer than he could have made in his mortal life.

Nick, atop Jazz, was lost in thought. His heart ached for the unicorns that were trapped deep at the bottom of the crater. The tower was now completely down and out of sight. Silence had replaced the crashing and rumbling sounds made by the rocks as they collapsed upon one another. The dust still rose up from the center of the crater in silent billowing clouds.

Far, far below a soft glow could be seen pulsating from the final embers and molten rocks.

Nick's heart welled up within him and he felt like it might choke him. *Jazz, we must do something to save them*, he thought.

Jazz came to a controlled stop first trotting, then walking, then halting squarely on all four legs. *I hear your thoughts. What do you want to do?*

I want to bring them up and heal them.

Is this wise? queried Jazz, concern clearly communicated through his thoughts.

I don't know, but I cannot go on and leave them there.

Remember, they chose this course for themselves, Nicholas.

Yes, that is true, said Nick slowly and thoughtfully, *but I can't escape the feeling that we must help them.*

We have expended a lot of power already and will undoubtedly need much more before we return to Celestia. To save them would require a great deal from our stores of love. You leg is injured. You are in need of healing yourself. Bethany, too, needs more of your power.

I have thought of that.

And you still feel that we must do this?

I do.

Then let us begin.

The boy and the horse turned toward the crater as one.

"What are you doing?" asked Bethany with fear in her voice.

Nick wrapped his arms tightly around her to help her feel secure. "We are going to save Hasbadana's guards."

Bethany stiffened. "Why would you do that?"

"We are doing this because we have pledged to use our power for good and to serve those in need. I cannot leave them where they are."

"But they were willing to leave me trapped as a prisoner for eternity. Why shouldn't they be treated the same way?" asked Bethany.

"Love does not seek revenge. Love seeks to forgive," whispered Jazz as he turned and looked at her with his big brown eyes.

Bethany, feeling shamed, lowered her head. "You see my unworthiness."

"No, I see your lack of training and confidence. We will replace that with the power of love," said Jazz as he nuzzled her foot with his nose. She reached down and stroked the big head in appreciation.

Nick and Jazz turned their attention back to the task they had set before themselves. Combining their power, with Nick as the spokesman, they focused their concentration on the bottom of the crater, the base of which they could not even see. "Stones at the floor of the crater, I command you to release the unicorns that lie beneath you." From the depths of the crater, a rumbling sound arose and echoed against the walls of the abyss. They envisioned stone after stone moving away from what must be an enormous pile of rubble. When the sound stopped, Jazz and Nick knew that the unicorns beneath were now uncovered. Their broken bodies were now free from their rocky prison. Yet Nick and Jazz were sure that the unicorns were still trapped at the bottom of the crater, too weak to escape without assistance.

Nick paused. He had never commanded an animal, much less a unicorn, before. Uniting their power once more, Nick spoke loudly and firmly, "Unicorns, I command your bodies to be lifted up from your grave and brought to us."

They waited for what seemed like an extraordinarily long time. Nick blinked his eyes and intensely stared into the cloud of smoke and dust. Silently, the form of a horse seemed to materialize before his eyes. Another and another appeared and moved through the air toward them.

Jazz stepped back, his ears reflexively pinned back against his head. Just as quickly, his ears turned forward again. Thirteen bent and broken unicorn bodies were laid out in front of them. Moans and groans could be heard coming from the dark motionless bodies. All of the dark unicorn's eyes were closed.

Nick slipped off of Jazz's back and cautiously approached the nearest unicorn. He kneeled beside him. "I am here to help you," he said as he reached out his hand and placed it on the unicorn's shoulder. The body that lay on the ground in front of him was cold and stiff yet Nick could tell it had previously been quite strong and muscular. The unicorn's flesh shivered at the warmth of his hand.

Nick kept his hand in place and let his eyes scan the body. The unicorn had a compound fracture of its foreleg and his spine was bent in an unnatural position. Open wounds covered the animal's neck, barrel, and flanks. A silver liquid oozed from the wounds. The internal injuries were undoubtedly as severe. Nick placed both hands upon each injury, commanding it to be healed. Intense light radiated from his fingertips. All the colors of the rainbow flowed into each injury. Next he moved his hands gently over the entire large, cold, angular body, sending the power of his love into the once-beautiful animal. Gradually, the groaning stopped and the unicorn slept.

One by one, Jazz and Nick worked over each of the thirteen bodies. When Nick, exhausted from his labors yet filled with the warmth that comes from serving others, reached the last unicorn, the dark beast slowly raised its head. Looking at Nick with fear in its eyes, the unicorn spoke in a quiet, weak voice, "Why are you doing this? We had come to destroy you and yet here you are saving us. Why?"

"Bethany asked me the same question," said Nick with a warm smile on his face. "I'll give you the same answer I gave to her: I am doing this because we have promised to use our power for the good of others," Nick replied solemnly.

"I don't understand that," said the unicorn dropping its head heavily back to the ground.

Nick began humming the song Shema had taught him as he set to work on the last unicorn.

Bethany was seated on the ground a short distance away and was watching all that Nick and Jazz were doing. When the last unicorn was healed, she walked slowly over to Nick and helped him stand up. She put her arms around him and hugged him. No words needed to be said for it was obvious that she finally understood the power of love.

Nick and Jazz were weak from their efforts. Bethany walked with them a short distance away from the sleeping unicorns. They sat down on the cold, dark ground which was now lit by their own light. Once they sat down, the pain in Nick's leg returned with a vengeance and he moaned and grimaced.

"In our rush to heal the unicorns, we forgot about your injury," said Jazz with concern in his voice. "I am so sorry."

Nick gritted his teeth but brushed off Jazz's concern with a quick motion of his hand. Bethany moved over to him and tore back the fabric of his pants, revealing an ugly gash down the side of his leg. But there was no blood. Just as Nick had noticed with the unicorns, where one would expect to see dark red blood, there was instead a thick, silver liquid—in some places still oozing, in other places coagulated. Nick and Bethany stared in shock.

Gently, Jazz answered their unspoken questions. "Your body no longer contains blood. That is one of the changes that took place when the unicorns made you immortal." Nick looked up at Jazz, surprise still on his face. Jazz summoned the last bit of strength within him to heal the large gash on Nick's leg.

"Thank you, Jazz," said Nick as he marveled at the speed with which his ugly wound healed. He turned toward Jazz and stroked the gelding's large head.

Nick suddenly became aware of how hungry he was. The young man and his horse had not eaten for a long time and they had used a lot of energy. He called forth what power he had left to summon water from the ground and fruit from the barren trees. Bethany watched, wide-eyed, as the sticks overhead brought forth apples, plums, peaches and cherries. She jumped up, laughing, and picked fruits until her arms were full. She brought them back to Nick and Jazz and picked some more to enjoy herself. Meanwhile, Jazz commanded the ground around him to bring forth grass so that he could stay resting where he was. He tore mouthfuls of sweet green grass and chewed happily.

Strength began to spread throughout their bodies. With their energy renewed, Nick surveyed their patients. All of a sudden, a thought entered his mind. *Shouldn't there be one more unicorn? There were Hasbadana's two guards that came into the room with him and the twelve we watched cross the bridge.*

"You're right, Nicholas, there were fourteen others. What do you make of that?"

"Perhaps I gave up too soon," Nick said. Adrenaline pumped through his veins. He sprang to his feet and hurried to the edge of the crater. Using an authoritative voice, Nick shouted into the dark pit. "Crater, I command you to yield up the last unicorn." His voice echoed down the chasm's stone walls. Nick, with Jazz now standing beside him, waited. Nothing happened. Nick turned and looked at Jazz with a perplexed expression. He tried again. The words echoed back and forth for a second time, but nothing more happened.

"Apparently, we miscounted," said Jazz while rubbing his head against Nick's arm.

The two friends, now convinced that they had recovered all the injured unicorns, turned and walked back to where Bethany now lay sleeping on the ground. Nick called forth a warm, wool blanket to cover her. Jazz settled down on a bed of straw and Nick sat beside him. He leaned his back against Jazz's warm shoulder and immediately fell asleep. Jazz wrapped his head and neck around him and slept as well.

The darkness deepened. Everyone, humans, horse, and unicorns, slept peacefully, their bodies gathering much-needed strength. Unbeknownst to any of them, and far behind, another unicorn by the name of Shazba struggled to the top of the crater's edge, turned and began galloping in the opposite direction from where the little group rested.

~ chapter 17 ~
Battle

orning arrived in the Dark Kingdom as cold, drab, and dark as ever. The wind continued to blow from all directions at once and an overwhelming silence pressed upon Nick's ears. The smell of smoke still hung in the air. The desolate land that surrounded them left him feeling isolated. Nick had no idea how far they needed to go, but he remembered that they had traveled a long way before arriving at their present location.

He stretched every limb before sitting up. He was taken aback to see that he was the last one awake. Bethany was gathering more fruit from the leafless trees. Jazz was bringing each of the unicorns grass and water for their breakfast.

Nick jumped up and brushed the straw from his tunic and out of his hair. "Good morning, everyone," he said mustering up the most enthusiasm possible in this bleak and foreboding place.

All of the unicorns turned to look at him. The two Clydesdales who had been Hasbadana's bodyguards lifted their large heads and turned toward him. Nick noticed how enormous and ominous their horns were. He stiffened as he watched the two of them walk toward him in perfectly synchronized steps, the feathering around their hooves flowing elegantly. They stopped in front of him.

"Master Nicholas," one said, while they both bowed so deeply that their massive horns touched the ground. "My name is Salamite and this is Portlas. We stand before you as your grateful servants. We will be eternally indebted to you and Jazz for rescuing us after having been abandoned to a stony prison by Hasbadana." He uttered the last word as though it hurt his mouth to say it.

Portlas joined in. "We are painfully aware that Hasbadana deserted us for his own purposes," he said with a sneer. He shook his head, snorted, and pawed the ground stridently.

"And you, who we had been taught was our enemy, interrupted your own flight to freedom to expend the time and power necessary to heal us," continued Salamite.

By this time, all of the unicorns had ceased eating and were moving closer to Nick. "We, as soldiers of the Dark Kingdom, have counseled together and it is our united decision that we will abandon our old lord, even as he abandoned us, and will commit our lives to your safety," said Portlas, acting as spokesman for all of the unicorns.

At this, one by one, each unicorn reared up on its powerful hind legs until all stood in a circle around Nick and Jazz. With thirteen horns pointing high in the air, the unicorns let out a loud, deep whinny that resonated off the stone walls of the canyon, on the edge of which they had rested for the night, and broke the silence of this new day into thousands of pieces.

They lowered themselves back onto all four legs, tossing their heads, manes flying and tails swishing. The first Clydesdale, who had identified himself as Salamite, turned toward his small army. "We must move with alacrity. We all know Hasbadana's ways. He will not wait long to regroup and prepare an attack against us. We must escort Master Nicholas safely to the Animal Kingdom. Hopefully we can stay ahead of him. Swiftly, my friends, swiftly! We can wait no longer," he commanded, his voice growing louder and the words coming faster with each command.

The urgency in his voice as he took command made Nick apprehensive. Jazz was obviously feeling the same way for he trotted over to Bethany and scooped her up on his back with his head and neck. Nick ran to join them and jumped up onto Jazz's back behind Bethany.

The thirteen guards arranged themselves into a "V" formation in front of Jazz and leaped forward into a ground-covering gallop. Jazz followed. The dark unicorns were accustomed to the terrain and were soon outpacing the gelding. Jazz struggled to keep up but found himself stumbling frequently on the stones and roots that interrupted the surface of the ground at irregular intervals. The two Clydesdales who were in the lead turned their heads as they ran, noticed that they were leaving their charges behind, and forced themselves and their little troop into a slower gallop. After several strides, Jazz caught up and managed to keep up with the new pace.

Nick forced himself to keep his eyes open as boulders and skeleton trees whizzed by. He and Bethany, both experienced riders, kept their balance whenever Jazz stumbled over the rocks or roots on the uneven ground.

On and on they ran, the dark unicorn Clydesdales leading the way. Not once did Nick suspect their intentions were anything but noble. Something about the tone of their voices told him that their sincerity and loyalty could be trusted. Something about their beings had changed. There was a new softness in their eyes and just a hint of sparkle. Nick was convinced that they were now his loyal friends.

For what must have been several hours, Nick caught glimpses of Jazz's former hoofprints glowing ahead of the leaders. By the time Nick and Jazz reached them, the hoofprints in the dust had been scattered to the winds by the leaders' pounding hooves. But Nick was confident that they were going back the way he and Jazz had come.

Eventually, the Clydesdales and their followers stopped for a respite. Jazz called forth water from the ground. They eagerly watched as the water formed a small pool from which they could all drink. Nick and Bethany slipped off of Jazz's back. Bethany used her hands like a groomer's curry comb to massage the gelding's tired muscles. Jazz stood still, eyes closed, enjoying the rubdown.

Salamite and Portlas stood to one side, constantly looking around them while they whispered together. Nick could not hear what they were saying, but the tension in their bodies and the sweat on their necks told him that they were less confident than they desired to portray to their companions.

The rest was short-lived. As soon as each creature had taken a drink and their heart rates had slowed, the Clydesdales called everyone into position. Salamite and Portlas trotted over to where Nick, Bethany, and Jazz stood. They both bowed before the two humans before they stood and solemnly looked from one to the other.

"Master Nicholas," began Salamite, "Portlas and I have been discussing the best route to take. Thus far, we have been following the same path on which you came in search of Bethany. We are aware that Hasbadana had his followers track you throughout your journey into the Dark Kingdom. We fear that he will be expecting you to return the same way. He will probably be lying in wait somewhere up ahead. We have concluded that the best course of action at this point would be to take another route, one that, perhaps, he won't anticipate. We would like to turn to the east and travel through the Valley of Corin. That will make it a longer journey, but we hope that by taking you that way, we can avoid any contact with Hasbadana's army."

Jazz turned and looked at Nick. *Can they be relied upon?*

I have been contemplating our situation carefully since last night and have concluded that we need help to find our way back home. There is nothing weak about trusting in others for that source of help. Yes, I believe they can be relied upon, responded Nick.

Nick bowed to Salamite and Portlas. "We are extremely grateful for your experience and guidance. We will follow your advice."

"Good. Then let's carry on," said Portlas. Both unicorns whirled around on their back legs and took their position at the point of the "V" formation. Turning to their followers they shouted, "We will be going through the Valley of Corin." They set off in a gallop and turned their cohorts to the right.

Nick turned his head to the left and watched until he could no longer see Jazz's glowing hoofprints. Now, he knew, he had completely turned his and his friends' safety over to these unicorns who, just a day before, had been Hasbadana's followers. He shivered slightly as a result of the sudden insecurity he felt.

Feeling Nick's body shiver, Bethany, though still drowsy, turned her head to look at him. "Are you alright?"

Not wanting to worry her, he simply said, "I'm just eager to be away from this place."

Bethany reached up a hand and stroked his cheek. With a warm smile she said, "We'll make it. I know we will."

Nick was surprised at the warmth of Bethany's hand and the feeling of comfort that her touch filled him with. He smiled as he looked into her eyes and considered the complete change of attitude that her words represented. Joy filled his heart as he saw the sparkle of light that now resided in them.

As they galloped through the eerie darkness, the sun disappeared. Nick was once again amazed that this familiar star, even though it could be seen as a round white orb in the sky, did not send any of its light into the Dark Kingdom. The darkness and coldness of this foreboding place remained the same, night or day. The dark unicorns were difficult to see. Jazz and Nick provided the only light. The wind continued to blow and the only sound was the pounding of the hooves and the strained breathing from thirteen unicorns and a horse. Puffs of warm steam escaped from twenty-eight nostrils. Nick smelled the sweat from Jazz's coat. This was truly a difficult journey for this beautiful horse with the big heart.

They turned and followed their leaders down a lengthy, sloping hillside and into the mouth of the Valley of Corin, a long, deep, and narrow canyon. Stone walls rose up on either side. Jazz snorted and his head came up as he looked from side to side. *I trust that Salamite and Portlas know where they are going and what they are doing,* Jazz thought.

They do, responded Nick, his faith and trust in his leaders finally returning.

Through the middle of the narrow valley ran a dry riverbed. Along this riverbed, the little group galloped at breakneck speed. The sound of the fourteen sets of hooves on the stone floor of the riverbed echoed off the walls of the canyon. The unicorns ran in rhythm with one another, their strides in perfect synchronization, their hoofbeats exactly together like the clog dancers in the performance of *Lord of the Dance* that Nick saw in New York during his Earth life.

Bethany was limp from exhaustion and totally dependent upon Nick to hold her in place on Jazz's back. Nick and Jazz strained their eyes to keep track of their surroundings as they ran. The light radiating from Nick and Jazz sent long shadows of their companions up the sides of the cliffs. Here they were sheltered from the otherwise ever-present wind. Finally, up ahead, Nick saw that the black walls of the canyon gave way to a gray opening. They were almost out of the narrow confines of the gorge.

Without warning, everything changed. The little band that had been running as one came to a sudden stop behind Salamite and Portlas. All ears were directed straight ahead. All nostrils were flaring. All sides were expanding and contracting with rapid, deep breathing.

"Master Nicholas, Jazz, drop back! Drop back!" yelled Salamite.

Nick squinted his eyes and stared ahead over the unicorn's heads. Barely visible across the opening of the canyon, Nick saw the dark bodies of many more unicorns. Instinctively, he reached into his pouch and placed a clover in his mouth, feeling it tingle as it dissolved.

Jazz, he thought with urgency, *take another clover. I think we should become invisible.* Nick reached into his bag and took out another clover and leaned forward, reaching his hand toward Jazz's head.

Jazz curled his head and neck back toward Nick's outstretched hand and took the clover with his lips. Immediately, they closed their eyes and drew in their light. All became dark around them, the shadows on the canyon walls disappeared. Jazz whirled, nearly unseating Bethany and Nick, and went quickly around to the side of their little army and over to the canyon wall.

Their thirteen protectors moved into a straight line across the canyon floor. They stopped and stood their ground, four feet planted firmly beneath each of them, their ears pinned back against their heads, the whites of their eyes visible even in the dark. Salamite raised his voice and called across the space that separated them from the dark unicorns that were blocking the exit of the canyon. "Comrades, we come in peace. We desire only to escort Nicholas, Jazz, and Bethany back to the Animal Kingdom where they belong. They mean us no harm in contrast to what we, and you, had been led to believe. In fact, they risked their lives to save us when the tower collapsed upon us. We owe them our protection."

From across the open space another voice responded in the same impassioned and articulate tones that Hasbadana was known to use. "I am Shazba." The thunderous voice echoed off the canyon walls, making the sound many times more threatening. "I now lead Hasbadana's true followers. The humans and the horse that you have with you are his prisoners. If you turn them over to us immediately, there will be no silver liquid shed and you can return to the ranks of Hasbadana's followers, although not in the positions of honor that you once held." He laughed as he added the last qualifier. He continued but this time his voice was lower and more menacing, "If you do not, we have been instructed to take all of you as prisoners."

"Ha!" exclaimed Portlas. "I've seen what Hasbadana does to the unicorns that cross him. I will fight as long as I have a body left before I will believe that lie."

Beside him the other unicorns nodded their heads, snorted, and stomped their feet in agreement. Nick and Jazz, with Bethany now fully awake, remained silently pressed against the canyon wall as they listened to the interchange.

Making another attempt to reason with the force blocking their path, Salamite spoke. "Shazba, I have known you since we chose to leave Celestia. I have no desire to harm you or any of our brothers. But I have pledged my honor to protect my charges."

"You pledged your honor to Hasbadana!" roared Shazba across the open ground, the words echoing off the cliff walls.

"He broke his part of that pledge first when he took our power and left us to suffer for eternity in a rocky grave!" Portlas yelled in retort.

"It was necessary that he escape so that he could continue to lead the rebellion. You should have felt honored to have been chosen to assist him," roared Shazba.

"Honored?!" responded Salamite, now letting the anger well up inside of him. He turned his head from side to side, with a derisive smile. "Did any of you feel honored when you were lying, bruised and broken, at the bottom of the crater?"

Each of his companions responded with sneers, snorts, and stomps. Slowly turning back to face Shazba, Salamite unhurriedly enunciated each word of his response as the volume of his voice rose. "I regret to tell you, Shazba, but not a one of us felt honored."

A loud, piercing whinny erupted from Shazba and reverberated down the entire length of the canyon, bouncing back and forth off the stone cliffs. "Then it shall be war!"

At that, Hasbadana's army, led by Shazba, reared high on their back legs and thrashed their front hooves through the air. They came down together. The minute their front feet hit the ground, they charged toward Nick's protectors.

The two Clydesdale commanders, both bigger and taller than any of the other unicorns, responded in kind. They lowered their heads, eyes squinting in anger, and charged toward the oncoming force without hesitation. Their horns were thicker and longer than any of the others' and they were able to make the first contact. Using their horns like a knight's lance they rammed into the first of Hasbadana's soldiers that crossed the divide between them. Deafening screams came from the two dark unicorns as Salamite and Portlas speared their chests and tossed them high in the air.

Almost immediately, the entire dark army was upon them. Salamite and Portlas moved through the horde, using their mighty horns like sickles, sending unicorn bodies flying in all directions as they cleared a pathway toward the back of the rabble.

The other eleven unicorn guards were more evenly matched with their opponents. They reared and struck with their front hoofs. They whirled and kicked. They dueled with their horns, sending sparks flying as their horns crashed together. When they moved in close enough, they tore at their opponent's flesh with their strong teeth and steel-like jaws.

Salamite and Portlas reached the back of the throng unscathed, turned around and started back through the battleground from the rear. Dark unicorns who were intent on their battle with the little army of guards, didn't notice their approach. Several of the enemy unicorns suddenly found themselves being lifted into the air as if by a forklift and tossed to the side. Like wild beasts, Salamite and Portlas worked as a team, all the while searching the mob for Shazba.

Shazba was circling the battlefield where his army outnumbered Nick's guards three to one. He was confident that the battle would be short-lived and victory would be theirs, even with the superior strength of Salamite and Portlas. His focus was on finding Nick, Jazz, and Bethany. He had not seen them, yet his senses told him that they were here. Ears pricked straight ahead and nostrils opened wide, he worked his way around the skirmish. Fortunately for Nick and Jazz, he had chosen to circle in a counter-clockwise direction. This was taking him farther away from where Jazz, Nick, and Bethany who, under the cloak of invisibility, remained waiting and watching, pressed tightly against the canyon wall.

Portlas was the first to spot Shazba. Portlas had always been the more aggressive and stronger of the two Clydesdales.

Portlas didn't hesitate for a moment. He turned his massive body, lowered his head, and charged. Shazba, also strong due to his Belgian breeding, was not as large or as nimble, and was distracted by his search for Nick. The leader of Hasbadana's army was caught by surprise. Portlas pierced his shoulder with his long horn, backed up, whirled, and kicked Shazba's side with both feet, knocking him onto the ground. Shazba had not seen any of this coming, but his loyalty to Hasbadana and his confidence in his own ability caused him to scramble immediately to his feet, ignoring the silver fluid that poured from his wound and down his front leg. He also disregarded the pain in his ribs from the kick and the fall. He lowered his head, aiming his horn toward his rival, and charged forward. Dodging and attacking, the two unicorns, once comrades in Hasbadana's army but now enemies, fought in a style reminiscent of duelers in a sword fight.

Salamite continued providing support for the rest of his troops, seeking out those who were outnumbered. He charged and rammed his old companions, now adversaries, sending them tumbling to their sides. The ear-piercing screams of pain filled the air and dust camouflaged the fight even more than the darkness.

Bethany yelled out in fear and desperation. "I can't tell who is winning! Isn't there something you can do to help? They are greatly outnumbered." She twisted her body around and beat her fists against Nick's chest. "You must do something!"

Nick felt as much horror as she did. He shook his head, not even realizing that, in his invisible state, she wouldn't be able to see him any more than he could see her. He groped through the air until he was able to grasp her wrists. He stared back at the mass of confusion that constituted the battle taking place before them. In his tenseness, he didn't even realize he was biting his bottom lip until he could taste something sweet. He reached up to wipe his mouth. He wrapped his arms tighter around Bethany and said, "Bethany, I can't even tell who is on our side in all this commotion. What can I possibly do?"

"I don't know, I don't know!" she screamed through clenched teeth, tears cascading down her cheeks.

Unexpectedly, Jazz said, "I have an idea. Dismount and climb up as high as you can on the rock wall and stay there. Nick, keep holding Bethany so she will stay invisible. Fast! Now!"

Nick slid off Jazz's back. Keeping one hand on Bethany, he let her slide down into his arms. As soon as they had dismounted, Jazz took off like a flash. Nick turned once in an attempt to watch him but immediately realized that his horse was still under the influence of the invisible clover. *I hope you know what you are doing*, he said to Jazz with his thoughts.

I do, too, was the hurried response.

Nick and Bethany began helping each other climb up the jagged rock wall. Nick struggled to keep one hand always on Bethany as she scaled the cliff ahead of him. When she had trouble reaching the next level, Nick pushed her up with all his strength. Suddenly, the stones in front of them shook and rumbled and rearranged themselves until they had formed themselves into a perfect staircase leading all the way up to the top of the precipice. Nick and Bethany stood up and started running up the steps. *Thanks, Jazz,* said Nick in his thoughts, amazed that Jazz had thought to build the staircase even as he charged into the disorder of the battle below them.

Behind them, in the dust and darkness, they could hear the battle as it raged on. The noise from the screaming, injured unicorns was sickening. All was mayhem. Suddenly, Nick heard Jazz speak to him in his thoughts: *Here they come.*

"Hurry, Bethany!" he said as he pushed her up the last few steps. They stepped onto the ground at the top of the staircase.

Behind them he could hear the sound of hooves climbing the stairs. After that, he heard something unfamiliar. Coming from the direction that they had originally entered the valley, Nick could hear a loud rushing and roaring sound. Nick and Bethany turned in unison. Tumbling down the canyon, a giant wall of water came crashing toward them. All of their guards were climbing up the staircase, one after the other, some limping from their injuries, but moving up, step by step, none the less.

Jazz, where are you? Are you coming? called out Nick in his mind.

Yes, I am behind the others, came his weak response.

Behind them, Hasbadana's army was running in all directions trying to find their opponents in the darkness. Suddenly, they became aware of the flash flood that was crashing toward them. They froze in fear. Shazba screamed his commands to draw his followers back under his control, "Follow me! I see them!"

The entire army turned and ran to follow their enemies to the safety of the stairs with Shazba in the lead. Just as Shazba leaped up toward the first step, his body stopped with a thud and fell back to the ground. He stood quickly and tried to leap onto the first step again. For a second time, he fell back, this time crashing into several of his minions. There was no time for a third attempt. The tumbling wall of water was upon them, sending them rolling and spinning through the canyon and depositing them in a jumbled, broken mass of intertwined legs, bodies, necks, and heads at the mouth of the canyon.

Jazz, still under the cloak of invisibility, stood from several steps up and watched the product of his work. He turned and stumbled up the rest of the steps to where Nick, Bethany, and their little band of loyal guards were waiting. When he reached the top of the staircase, Jazz collapsed.

chapter 18

Salamite

The moment Jazz's eyes shut and he hit the ground, he unconsciously released the light within him and became visible again. Nick, having released his own light and hearing Jazz's hoofbeats coming up the rock stairs, was awaiting his arrival. Nick rushed to the side of his beloved friend. He dropped to his knees and gently scooped up Jazz's large head onto his lap. Bethany knelt beside him, stroking Jazz's neck.

"What's the matter?" she asked, concern mixed with fear filling her heart and reflected in her voice.

"He's badly injured," said Nick, his voice trembling.

Salamite stepped up behind them. "Jazz worked his way through the battle to find each of your guards. One by one he sent them to the staircase, fighting off their opponents long enough to give them time to escape." With a chuckle he added, "Since Jazz was invisible, those poor soldiers couldn't figure out what was attacking them."

Becoming serious again, he continued, "Unfortunately, Jazz endured a lot of blows and kicks. But he kept on going, from guard to guard, until he had told all of us his plan for escape. Now it is he who must be rescued."

Nick looked up at Salamite, "Will your army be okay while I spend my time healing Jazz?"

"Oh, yes. I have surveyed the entire troop. None has suffered more than a flesh wound here and there. Nothing that cannot wait. Thank you for your continued concern for us. Is there anything we can do for you?"

"Just keep up your guard."

"That we will do. Hasbadana is not accustomed to defeat. He will not stay away for long," answered Salamite. The large Clydesdale unicorn turned around and returned to his fellow dark unicorns, leaving Nick and Bethany alone to heal Jazz.

Nick turned his full attention to his beloved horse. He looked over the large, muscled Hanoverian body. There were several open wounds, with the mysterious silver liquid flowing freely from them that needed immediate attention. Nick set Jazz's head carefully onto the ground and began working over his body. He had no trouble calling forth the power within him; in fact, his love seemed to pour forth from him like a hot flame. As he placed his hands over each wound, the intense rays of light from his fingertips had so much power that he had to consciously hold his hands still over each wound to keep them from bouncing around.

As his hands sent healing power into each injury, Nick watched with amazement as muscles grew back together and the flesh returned to its proper form and position. Nick's heart was filled with gratitude for the power the fairies had bestowed upon him.

While Nick worked over each part of Jazz's body, Bethany sat by the gelding's head, gently stroking it. How long Nick worked was impossible to say, but once he was sure that Jazz's body was healed, he sat back, resting his hands on his knees and bowing his head in gratitude and exhaustion.

Bethany stopped stroking Jazz's head and looked up at Nick. "Is he going to be all right?"

Nick let out a long breath of air, as though he had been holding his breath all this time. "Yes, he just needs some rest now." Taking in a large gulp of air and gathering his strength, he said, "I will go check on the unicorns. You stay here with Jazz, but keep your eyes open."

With great effort, Nick stood up. He found Salamite, who directed him to each of the unicorns that needed his help. Salamite was right. None of the unicorns were seriously injured and Nick was able to heal each of them without expending a great deal of additional energy. Still, when he was done with the last unicorn, he stumbled back to where Bethany continued to hold and caress Jazz's head and collapsed to the ground beside the gelding's sturdy back. He wasn't so much sleepy as he was physically depleted.

He laid his head against Jazz's side and let his mind wander back over the day's events. As he did so, he came to realize just what his amazing horse had accomplished. Jazz came up with the plan of how to save their friends. Jazz called forth the stone stairway out of the rock cliff. Jazz found each of their guards and directed them to safety while distracting each of the soldiers from Hasbadana's army long enough for them to retreat up the stairway. Jazz called forth the flash flood. And Jazz had been the last one to climb to safety after making sure that everyone else was out of harm's way.

Nick turned onto his side and wrapped an arm over the big, black body. He rested his head on the horse's shoulder and let himself relax against the gelding. He let his breathing match each breath that Jazz took. He let his heart beat together with his friend's. A feeling of gratitude filled his entire being for all that this horse meant to him. He became calm and was able to rest at last.

"Are you feeling okay, Nick?" asked Bethany in a whisper.

"I am now," was his response.

Salamite slowly approached the threesome. "May I rest with you?"

"Please join us," said Bethany, feeling comfortable around the unicorns for the first time.

Salamite curled his large legs beneath him and laid down on the stony surface of the plateau. He did not initiate any conversation.

Nick, finally gathering enough energy to talk, turned his head to face Salamite. "Salamite, can I ask you something?"

"Anything, Master Nicholas."

"Why did you become one of Hasbadana's followers?"

Salamite shifted his position slightly and looked off into the darkness. He let out a long sigh before he began. "You must understand that Hasbadana has a great gift of persuasion. His arguments seem to make complete sense initially. But after you have committed yourself to him and his ideas, his governing switches from persuasion to fiat. You see, once he has you under his control he takes all freedoms from you. You no longer have the freedom to choose for yourself. Your only option is to do as he commands."

"But what about his philosophy drew you to him initially?" interrupted Nick while Bethany sat silently looking from one to the other.

"While we were horses in Celestia, we were being trained to assist all of the animals. You understand what I am saying. You and Jazz have recently completed the same training in the schooling arena. Hasbadana was one of the horses selected to train to become a unicorn. He displayed remarkable skill and learned all of his lessons quickly. For a time, he was even serving as Urijah's personal assistant."

Nick stared at Salamite with a look of astonishment on his face.

"Yes, he could have been an exceptionally great unicorn. But something changed within his heart once we became unicorns and were sent through the mist to help our animal brothers and sisters. Hasbadana became very bitter as he witnessed the cruelty humans inflicted upon animals."

"I am aware that some humans are unkind to animals. But surely you realize that most humans are not," interrupted Nick again.

"Please do not be offended by what I have to say, but to Hasbadana, it was much too common. His heart became hard and his soul bitter. He became convinced that it should be the right of all animals to be free of human domination…and that it was the animals who rightfully should rule the world both in mortality and in immortality. Nothing that Urijah said could comfort or console him. He rebelled against Urijah when he could not convince the Lord of Celestia and his Council to follow his plan."

"What was his plan?" asked Nick cautiously.

"He wants to lead the animals on Earth to rebel against their human owners or, as he would say, 'oppressors,'" interjected Bethany.

"Yes, she is exactly right. Not what *was* his plan, it is more correct to say: what *is* his plan," added Salamite. "Once the animals have rebelled, he desires to return to Earth and rule as an immortal over all beings, both animal and human."

Nick was at a loss for words. This was beyond anything he could have imagined. Instantly he thought back over his mortal life, the people he had known and loved. The people he had observed. All of these people had been kind and loving to their animals. Indeed, horses lived much better and longer lives under the care of their human owners than the horses that had to try to survive in the wild. Yet there was no denying that many animals suffered under the hands of humans, whether through ignorance or intent he knew not.

"Do you feel this way about humans?" asked Nick, looking deeply into Salamite's eyes for the answer to his question.

"I am ashamed to say that I became a victim of Hasbadana's powerful influence. In fact, I became one of his most loyal followers. I was convinced that what he was telling me was true. I began to see humans as the source of all domination and cruelty toward animals. He had little trouble persuading me that animals are far superior in every way to humans. My mind was filled with his philosophy of how to reorder the world to make life better for the animals during their Earth life. As a result, I, along with all of the unicorns who desired to follow Hasbadana, was cast out of Celestia. Our powers that had been fueled by the love within us were lost when that love was replaced by hate and fear. We now draw our power from others. We have none of our own."

Nick had not noticed that all of the other unicorns had left their resting places and were now gathered around them, listening to the conversation. Salamite motioned his large bay head toward the unicorns. Nick looked around at them for the first time. "We are all drawn toward the light that radiates from you and Jazz. You have no idea how we have missed the feeling of living in the light."

Nick became acutely aware of Bethany. She sat stroking Jazz's head and crying softly. For the first time, he noticed that a faint glow was released from her skin. She was no longer dark like the unicorns. *Perhaps even the dark unicorns can regain their light*, he thought to himself.

"Why did Hasbadana take Bethany?" he asked, wanting to know more about this evil lord named Hasbadana.

"Hasbadana tried to learn all he could about humans. Bethany was the first human that had been brought into Celestia. He assumed that she had special powers that Urijah and the Council wanted to use. Hasbadana wanted to capture that power for himself."

"But I had no power," said Bethany, her voice quivering from her ready tears.

Salamite turned and looked directly at her. "That is not true. You had power, you were just weak. You certainly did not have any unusual powers of your own. Your power came from the love that Shema, oh, I believe you called her Lady, gave you. This only convinced Hasbadana all the more that his theory of animal superiority over humans was correct. He had no trouble draining you of what power you had by convincing you of your worthlessness. I am sorry to say that we all stood by and watched as he took from you what little love you had. He drained you of your natural kindness. He stole from you your empathy and compassion. He robbed you of your patience and loyalty. Everything of value he used to build up his own strength."

"I didn't realize I ever had those virtues."

"Oh, yes, you did and you still do, some in abundance. And you can have them back now that you are out from under Hasbadana's influence," responded Salamite, "as long as you refuse to let him darken your heart. You see, Bethany, he only has as much power over you as you let him have. You were weak and easy to manipulate, but he cast you off because he couldn't break you down completely. There was something in you that kept you strong enough to resist him. I know this because Portlas and I were always present when he confronted you. Frankly, you are quite amazing. You were able to resist him much better than any of us could."

"What kept you from resisting him?" Nick asked Salamite.

"As I said, for a long time I was convinced that what he desired for the Animal Kingdom was virtuous and noble. I truly had the same desires. However, it wasn't until he brought Bethany into the Dark Kingdom, and I was able to observe his attempts to manipulate her, that I was able to see what he had done to me...to all of us," he added.

He looked toward the other unicorns, some of whom were laying down, others standing. "Why didn't I do anything, you must be asking yourself? I asked myself the same things many times. I finally concluded that I have developed an overabundance of one virtue: loyalty." He paused and took a deep breath. "Master Nicholas, do you remember the circle of virtues that surround the schooling arena and that decorate the ceiling in the great room before the Council chambers?"

Nick nodded, encouraging Salamite to continue.

"They are always in a circle. I have decided that is for an important reason. There is no beginning and no end to a circle. All are equal in a circle."

Nick's mind went immediately to King Arthur and his Knights of the Round Table.

Salamite continued, "As further evidence of the importance of the equality of the virtues, recall, if you will, that the animals in the ceiling of the great room are constantly changing positions. They have no leader. They are all equally important. My weakness lies in the fact that I developed one virtue at the expense of the others. I let loyalty dominate my actions. To be truly great, I, and everyone else, need to develop all of the virtues equally. Unfortunately, I wasn't able to synthesize all of these thoughts while under Hasbadana's influence. I wasn't able to, that is, until I lay at the bottom of the crater under bone-crushing rocks, having been abandoned and discarded by the very being to whom I had given all my great abundance of loyalty."

Bethany looked up, her eyes shining and her mouth spread into the most beautiful smile Nick had ever seen. She gently set Jazz's head down, leaned forward onto her hands and knees and crawled over to where Salamite lay. She sat on her heels in front of him for a moment. With a sigh, she leaned forward and threw her arms around his neck.

A large smile spread across Nick's face. He watched as the light within Bethany began to glow brighter and brighter.

⊸ chapter 19 ⊸

The Dark Mist

After a long rest, Nick struggled up onto his feet. His body felt cold and stiff. He stretched his arms and rolled his shoulders in an attempt to loosen up. Bethany, who was curled up on a feather duvet a few feet away, followed his movements with her eyes before she whispered, "What are you going to do?"

"I feel restless. I need to start moving. I can't escape the feeling that Hasbadana is near. I'm going to see what I can do to prepare for our departure."

Nick busied himself bringing food to Bethany, and water, grass, carrots, and apples to all the unicorns. He continually glanced over to where Jazz lay sleeping on his side. He kept suppressing the nagging worry within him. Had he done enough to heal Jazz? Would Jazz recover? Nick kept working to keep his mind occupied.

The wind blew all around them. The darkness enveloped them. The silence surrounded them. Only the contented grazing of the unicorns on the grass that Nick had called forth from the ground made any sound.

At last, the words that Nick had been anxiously awaiting entered his head: *Nick, I'm awake.* Joy mixed with relief filled

Nick's heart. He turned and quickly ran to where Jazz's body lit the surroundings. Nick jumped on his back and threw his arms around both sides of Jazz's neck. Jazz turned his head and nuzzled his left foot.

"You're awake! How do you feel?" Nick asked with excitement in his voice.

"Great, thanks to you."

"Thanks to *me*? If it hadn't been for *you* we would all be Hasbadana's prisoners by now. What you did was awesome."

"Thank you, Master Nicholas, but I did nothing that you would not have done."

"If I had been able to think that fast! Oh, and don't call me 'Master,'" he said, giving Jazz a wink of his eye as he thought of his conversation with Salamite.

Bethany and Salamite came up and expressed their pleasure at Jazz's recovery. Bethany threw one arm around Jazz's neck and rubbed his face with her other hand. Immediately, Salamite became serious and turned everyone's attention back to the matter at hand. "If Jazz is feeling strong enough, I suggest we continue our journey immediately. I know Hasbadana will be planning another attempt to capture you. I would like to try to move out and stay ahead of him."

"Which way should we go to get off this plateau?" asked Nick.

"Portlas has been scouting the best route to take."

At that, Portlas approached and bowed to Jazz and Nick. "Jazz, let me speak for all of us when I thank you for once again coming to our rescue. It seems it is your guards that always need liberating," said Portlas. Jazz humbly acknowledged the expression of gratitude with a slight nod of his head.

"Now," continued Portlas, "I have been exploring this plateau. The entire highland actually slopes gently to the east. If we follow the plateau in that direction, it will drop us back to the dark plains on which we were traveling when we entered the Valley of Corin. We can then turn back to the south and proceed to the Animal Kingdom."

"Well done, Portlas. Thank you," said Nick. Turning to Jazz, he said, "Jazz, once you have had some sustenance, we will depart." He smiled at himself as he realized he was beginning to sound like a unicorn in his manner of speech. He slid off of Jazz's back, called forth aromatic green grasses from the infertile ground, and commanded an apple tree to sprout and produce crisp red apples in a matter of seconds. A pool of cool, refreshing water bubbled up at their feet. Jazz busied himself consuming his feast.

They took little time to prepare. Nick mounted Jazz and Bethany mounted Salamite. She gave Nick and Jazz a big smile as she waved to them from the back of the enormous Clydesdale unicorn. All of the unicorns took their positions and the entire entourage took off at a gallop, following the downward slope of the plateau.

Once down from the highlands, they turned back to the south. They were again running through the skeleton trees. Each of the unicorns had to weave their own path through the dark, dead, dreary forest.

Jazz and Nick followed the route Salamite and Bethany had taken. The light Nick and Jazz emitted radiated out in all directions. Nick watched ahead of him as his light illuminated the backs of Salamite and Bethany, sending shadows in front of them as they ran. *It must be a new sensation for Salamite to be following his shadow in this otherwise shadowless land,* he thought to himself.

Jazz acknowledged Nick's thoughts by bobbing his head up and down.

Nick's attention turned to Bethany. He watched with admiration as her thin, frail body flowed like liquid velvet as she moved in rhythm with Salamite's canter. A feeling of warmth filled his entire body as he watched her ride the unicorn across the rocky plain of the Dark Kingdom. The warmth and light he felt was in conspicuous contrast to the cold and dark beyond them.

As time and distance continued to pass, Nick became increasingly hopeful that Hasbadana would leave them alone and let them return to the Animal Kingdom in peace. Jazz, hearing his thoughts, cautioned him not to be too optimistic.

Portlas moved over beside them and let out a loud whinny. Nick turned his head and looked at him quizzically. "Look ahead, I can see the border of the Animal Kingdom, Master Nicholas," Portlas said to Nick.

Nick looked straight ahead. He could just make out a ribbon of light beyond the glow cast from their bodies, where before there had been only darkness. A rush of joy, excitement, and anticipation filled him. *Look ahead, Jazz! I can see the light. We're almost home.*

The little band galloped forward with renewed enthusiasm. Suddenly, everything changed. Without warning, a black mist descended upon the little group. Gone was the beacon of light that had drawn them forward. Gone was the hope and excitement that had stirred their souls. Now there was only darkness and confusion.

The mist of darkness clung to them, pressing against their bodies like a boa constrictor trying to squeeze the life out of them. "Keep your mouths closed," Salamite was able to shout, before he dropped his head and coughed violently to clear his throat of the dark mist that had entered his mouth and throat in the short time it took to speak his command. All of the unicorns stopped, some bumping into one another. No one could see. Even the light that shone from Jazz and Nick was swallowed up in the darkness as though a black cloak had been thrown over them.

Nick turned his head one way, then another, trying to see something—anything. He could feel Jazz beneath him, the gelding's body tense. *Jazz, I can't see anything. I can hardly breathe.*

This is some magic spell. I am going to follow my senses to try to find Salamite.

Nick's thoughts went immediately to Bethany. He could not see anything, as though he were in a cave with his lantern burned out. He covered his mouth to protect his throat from the encroaching mist and called out, "Bethany! Where are you? Are you all right?"

"I'm here, I'm here. Come find me," said Bethany with panic in her voice. She immediately started coughing to clear her throat and thwart the mist in its attempt to choke her.

Jazz moved cautiously forward in the direction of the sound of Bethany's coughing, nostrils flared sucking in both mist and the scent of the other unicorns. Within a few strides his nose was pressing against the cold body of the huge Clydesdale. Jazz sneezed to clear his airways of the mist.

"Hasbadana," was all Salamite uttered.

Suddenly, as if in response, a voice penetrated the dark mist. "I tire of this little game." The words entered their ears through the thickening black mist. A low, deep laugh vibrated through the darkness. Stark and savage images of his enemy filled Nick's brain and he shuddered violently.

The cruel, cold voice spoke again but this time with a more consolatory tone. "Ah, my young friends, compassion fills my heart for you. I have concluded that your rebellion is simply out of weakness and ignorance. Your behavior is the result of your limited perspective. Yes, indeed, you are merely the victims of your own misconceptions. You, Nicholas and

Jazz, have lived your lives under a cloak as dark as this mist. You cannot see things as they really are. Let me," at this point he chuckled, "*enlighten* you!" His voice rose in volume. "We unicorns were designed and destined to become the rulers of all the human and animal kingdoms. The order of the world has been mistakenly inverted. But find your joy in this: together we have not only the opportunity, but the duty to correct the error," his voice rising to a crescendo.

All the unicorns stood in their individual prisons of darkness, frozen to the spot, none daring to move and hesitating to even breathe.

Hasbadana continued in a consciously controlled comportment. "The choice is yours, but you must realize that I cannot let you depart from my kingdom. You may reside here with me as my comrades, even elevated to the position of counselors or," he paused momentarily before continuing, "as my prisoners. But you must make the choice." He laughed with derision at the use of the word "choice."

"Yes…choice! Such an important principle! Ah, but think not for a moment of the latter option. Think only of the magnificence of the first and be not tempted to despair." Hasbadana lowered his voice in a reassuring manner. "You need only acquiesce to my will. Simply persuade yourself that the opportunity I offer you will be in the best interest of both humans and animals. With my plan, we can guarantee that all living creatures, my animals and your humans, can live in peace and prosperity. No more pain, no more cruelty, no more sorrows."

For a moment there was a thick, penetrating silence. Nick, Bethany, Jazz, and their unicorn escorts waited with trepidation. They were trapped in this mist of darkness, afraid to move and not knowing what to do. The reassuring tone of voice returned through the mist. "You have been guests in my kingdom. You have had the unique opportunity to see firsthand my greatness and my glory. Here in my kingdom you can revel in what you might perceive to be austerity but is actually realism and, yes, even dignity. Mine is a life you can learn to relish." He paused. "Now, enough of my words. What say you to my generous offer? Before you respond, know that I will not be so magnanimous another time. My patience, as abundant as it is, has found its end."

Silence followed.

In Nick's mind the silence was replaced by Jazz's words. *You have been given the power of love, not of fear. You can resist his evil plan.*

But if we deny him, what will become of us? Of Bethany, of Salamite, Portlas, and the others?

I know not. I know only that the choice is clear. We must always use our power for the good of all.

Great strength and conviction filled every part of Nick's body and he spoke into the dark mist, not even bothering to cover his mouth. "Hasbadana, you are a deceiver. To follow you would be to abandon all that I am, all that I can become. I would rather be your prisoner for all eternity than to join in your evil designs to control and conquer." When he was done speaking, he ducked his head and coughed violently.

A great squealing whinny reverberated through the oppressive mist. Hasbadana spoke with a voice so loud it shook the dark ground on which they cowered. "So be it. And so you will know that I can be ingenuous, let me say this: You are nothing but a cipher. To me you are primarily food. My aim is to absorb your light and power to enhance my own. I have no further use for any of you beyond that."

A great and wicked laugh filled the mist and all of the unicorns shook their heads and snorted to rid themselves of the painful, piecing sound. Nick and Bethany covered their ears and squeezed their eyes shut.

In an instant, all was silent. The mist became colder and heavier. Every creature in the little party of rebels waited, fearing to move, fearing to even breathe.

Nick reached his hand to the side, flailing in the darkness until his hand made contact with Salamite's strong, solid body. The unicorn jumped to the side but, realizing that it was Nick who had touched him, moved back until he was once again pressed against Jazz's body. Nick slid from Jazz's back onto Salamite and scooted forward until he was close behind Bethany. He wrapped his arms around her and she crumpled against him and started to cry. Her crying sounds made all of the other unicorns uneasy and they shuffled over toward them until the entire group was a tightly knit pack, reminiscent of emperor penguins trying to gain shelter from the vicious biting winds of an Antarctic winter.

There, the little group stood, awaiting their fate. They had no idea what form that fate might take nor how long they would have to wait for its arrival. But in a strange way, they were gaining strength from the knowledge that they would face whatever came their way together. Nick surprised himself at the attitude of calm that filled him. He thought of the stories he had heard of the prisoners during Earth's Vietnam War who were incarcerated in the "Hanoi Hilton." In such dire circumstances, those prisoners found strength beyond their own, a power within them that they didn't know they possessed. Nick knew that the dark mist was suffocating his light externally but he could feel that strength increasing internally.

At that moment, a thought entered his mind: *Gloforia.*

What are you thinking, Nicholas? whispered Jazz in his mind.

Gloforia. I believe that she can help us. Nick projected a vision of the glorious eagle to Jazz's mind.

What can she do?

I don't know, but I have the overwhelming impression that she can help us. I will call her and see if she can hear me.

Nick stiffened his body and took in a deep breath. "Gloforia," he called out loud. The sound echoed as it bounced off the walls of mist that entombed them. "Gloforia!" he called again, with all the power within him. The young boy coughed and gagged on the mist that filled his throat. But this time, the sound seemed to escape their prison walls and move out into the freedom of the darkness around them.

Let us wait and see if she answers you, thought Jazz to Nick.

The mist pressed even tighter against them and all the unicorns leaned even closer together. Nick waited for an answer in any form from his friend. Around him, the unicorns snorted and shuffled their feet but, for quite a while, there was no other sound.

Nick caught his breath. His ears strained to hear any sound through the mist, but he was certain he had detected a noise. Jazz and Salamite, too, raised their heads, pushing against the mist that bore down on them, and pointed their ears forward.

Do you hear it? thought Nick.

Yes. Something is approaching. But I have no idea what it could be.

Listening carefully once again, Nick waited. Excitement filled his breast as he heard the sound again, louder this time, and clearer, too. What he heard was the sharp-pitched scream of a raptor, the call of an eagle.

As clear as any shepherd's call to his sheep, every creature in their assemblage heard the voice beyond their confinement. "It is I, Gloforia. Follow the sound of my voice. I will lead you."

Nick covered his mouth with his hand and shouted out a command. "Follow the sound of the eagle."

Salamite waited until Nick had crawled back onto Jazz and the boy and his horse had pushed past him. The little group struggled and fought their way through the asphyxiating cloud. At first, they shuffled like surgery patients taking their first walk down the hospital hall. Soon they became more confident and their steps became bolder and strides longer. The black mist tried to push them back and was unrelenting in its counterattack, but the unicorns, their heads bowed as they pushed against the pressing wall of mist, continued to follow Jazz. The big gelding moved forward, following the sound of Gloforia's screeches.

Gloforia acted as the huntsman at a foxhunt. The huntsman uses the sounds from his horn to send the hounds to the right or to the left. Gloforia did the same, keeping the little group in the black prison moving in the right direction with her calls. Slowly and persistently, the group pushed their prison walls of mist forward, step by step, toward the light they could not see. Only faith in the call of Gloforia kept them on track.

Suddenly, the black mist started to dissolve like a snowflake melting on the warm sidewalks of New York. Encouraged by their apparent success, the group pushed forward, stronger and faster. The mist responded by dissolving more quickly. Without warning, the mist disappeared and the group stood surrounded by warmth and light. They were safely within the confines of the Animal Kingdom.

chapter 20

home again

Light! Glorious, all-encompassing light! Nick squeezed his eyes tightly together. After so many days in darkness, his eyes were straining to protect themselves from the brightness of the light in the Animal Kingdom. Bethany covered her eyes as she waited for her pupils to find a comfortable diameter. Jazz and the unicorns curved their necks and tucked their heads against one another.

When Nick was comfortable enough to open his eyes, he looked around. Above him, Gloforia ceased her circling and swooped down and landed on his head. Nick laughed and reached his hand up to stroke the huge bird's strong body. "Gloforia, you came!"

She brushed her beak through his hair affectionately. "I told you I would always be there to help you."

"But you came into the Dark Kingdom. Weren't you frightened?"

"When you called for me, I didn't think about fear. As Jazz is always reminding you, we have been given the spirit of love, not fear. Since the unicorns are not allowed to enter the Dark Kingdom, I knew it was my responsibility to save you.

My, my, you certainly had yourself in a predicament," said the eagle with a chuckle.

"Yes, I did get more than I bargained for, that's for sure!" Nick laughed.

"Hasbadana's spell was strong enough to envelop your light. I did not realize that he had become so powerful," said a familiar voice from beside them.

Nick and Jazz turned their heads quickly. They were filled with excitement and joy to see Mastis standing there, smiling at them. Gloforia flapped her long wings once and rose into the air, letting out a joyous screech as she did so.

"Mastis!" shouted Nick, surprising everyone, including himself, at the volume of his exclamation. "We did it, Mastis. We rescued Bethany." Nick jumped off Jazz's back and ran to hug Mastis.

The beautiful unicorn encircled Nick with his neck and head. "You have done a remarkable thing, my young foals. I am so proud of you both."

Shema stepped up beside Mastis, but her eyes looked beyond them to the frail young girl sitting on the back of the giant dark unicorn. Noticing the silence that suddenly surrounded them and sensing the eyes upon her, Bethany slowly forced her eyes open and turned her head toward them. For a moment, she sat frozen in place, but then a huge smile spread across her face. "Lady," she whispered, joy emanating from her entire body.

Salamite kneeled down onto his left, front knee, and Bethany slid onto the ground.

"Lady," she whispered again as she stood by Salamite's shoulder.

Shema stepped forward and nuzzled Bethany to her golden neck, her long, pearly-white mane falling over Bethany's face. The delicate, young girl wrapped her thin arms around Shema's neck and embraced her with what little strength she had.

"Bethany, you are back. You are safe now. I will never, no never, let Hasbadana take you away from me again."

Bethany laughed as tears flowed down her cheeks. "Oh, don't worry about that. He doesn't want me. I was of no use to him. But Nicholas and Jazz rescued me. I owe my life to them," she said. She turned her face toward Nick without letting go of Shema's neck and said, "I can never thank you enough."

"Nor can I," added Shema. "Nor can I."

Nick swept his arms out in front of him, motioning toward the little army of dark unicorn soldiers. Except for Salamite's bow, the band of guardians had not moved during the entire welcome. They stood with their heads down, huddled tightly together. Their angular bodies and dark countenances stood out in sharp contrast to the radiant, sparkling glow emanating from Mastis and Shema's full, rounded bodies. Their eyes remained shut. They waited, united in their trepidation. They had no way of knowing what kind of reception they would receive here in the land of their enemies. Salamite and Portlas had not planned upon entering the Animal Kingdom. Indeed, they had not planned beyond the immediate task of helping Nicholas, Jazz, and Bethany escape. Now they found themselves in the land from which they had once been cast out.

Sensing their concern, Nick spoke up. "These are our friends. They risked their lives to save us." He turned and looked from Mastis to Salamite then back to Mastis and pleaded: "We must keep them safely here in the Animal Kingdom. If we force them to return to the Dark Kingdom, Hasbadana will enslave them and feed upon them to build up his own strength and power."

Mastis stepped forward, boldly and confidently approaching Salamite.

Salamite, sensing his presence, raised his head, yet his eyes remained shut. Mastis pressed his muzzle against the dark unicorn's and breathed softly into his nostrils.

Salamite returned the greeting.

"Salamite, my brother, I am so happy to see you again. A part of my heart went with you when you left Celestia. Now my heart is full and complete once more."

Tears squeezed out from Salamite's closed eyes. "I have been in the darkness so long I had forgotten how much I once loved the light. Now that light pains me and my eyes are blinded to it. Though I can not see you with my eyes, Mastis, I can see you with my heart. I thought I had forgotten how to love, but how wrong I was." He paused and pressed his muzzle once again tightly against Mastis' and blew cold breath into the unicorn's nostrils. Lowering his voice, he added, "It matters not to me what you choose to do with us. This moment back in the light has made our return worth the struggle."

The two unicorns, one light and sparkling in the sun, the other cold and dark, stood muzzle to muzzle and Mastis spoke once more. "It is neither my position nor my responsibility to pass judgment upon you. It is only up to me to love you and that I do, fully and unconditionally. Urijah and the Council will decide your fate and how you must repent of your crimes. We will take you to them. However, I am sure that your acts of heroism concerning your protection of our young foals will play well for you in their decision."

Mastis greeted each of the unicorns, one by one, welcoming them back into the light. Next, he called for Jazz and Nick, "We need to heal our friends before we attempt to lead them to Celestia," he said.

The dark unicorns, whose eyes had atrophied from lack of light, could not endure the intense, all-encompassing light of Celestia. One by one, each was lovingly healed by Mastis, Shema, Jazz, and Nick.

They timidly opened their eyes, blinked several times, and looked around. After having been away from the light for so long, all they could do was stand in awe of the sights that surrounded them.

"Everything is so beautiful!" whispered one.

"I had forgotten what light looked and felt like," exclaimed another.

"How could we have ever left this behind?" asked a third.

Others just stood silently, tears running down their cheeks.

Salamite lifted his head. He tossed his long forelock to one side of his horn as he breathed in the warm air and looked around for Portlas. Portlas stood to the side of the group. His eyes were now healed and he was silently looking around him. Salamite noticed him look back to where they had come from, to where the light meets the dark. A splinter of fear swept into Salamite's heart as he watched his brother gaze toward the wall of darkness, but his attention was drawn back to Mastis and he forced his concern to the back of his mind.

As was characteristic of Mastis, he was the first to draw everyone's attention to the matter at hand. "Now, my friends, we have a long way to go before we return to Celestia. Shall we begin?"

Nick swung his leg up and over Jazz's back and wrapped his fingers through the thick mane. Bethany chose to climb aboard the familiar back of the horse she had known and loved: the unicorn named Shema. The two friends, now reunited, couldn't have been happier. Portlas came up beside Salamite and rubbed his friend's neck with his muzzle. Salamite turned and smiled at him. The army of dark unicorns fell in behind as the entire group followed Mastis.

High above them, Gloforia let out a loud, long cry, flapped her strong wings and led the way.

They all set off in a smooth, rocking gallop, their feet hardly touching the ground between strides. Nick watched the reaction of the animals as they passed by with some amusement. Their first response was one of joy and excitement as they recognized Mastis. But at the sight of the dark unicorns, the animals shied away. While none of them had seen a dark unicorn, their legends had told of the unicorns' existence, their power, and their evil mission. The cold darkness that their bodies emitted made them easy to recognize. The younger and smaller animals ran and hid. The older and larger held their ground, but stood frozen in place. *Surely*, they were thinking, *Mastis must know what he is doing bringing them here.*

Nick smiled to himself as he listened to their thoughts.

When they arrived at the familiar beaver hut for a night's rest, the animals awaiting their return were shocked at the size of the group that arrived. The bravest of the beavers approached them when they came to a stop. "My, but your group has grown. We were not expecting so many of you. I'm afraid the log hut we constructed will not accommodate such a large number of unicorns."

Salamite stepped up and the beaver quickly shuffled his feet backward several yards. "Do not worry, kind host," said Salamite in his softest voice, though lacking the melodic, musical tones of the unicorns of Celestia. "We will be quite comfortable outside. We are quite accustomed to the, uh… darkness."

Behind him the dark unicorns smiled at one another.

"Oh…oh yes, of course," stammered the beaver. "Please do make yourselves comfortable." He gave them a slight nod of his head then cast a questioning look toward Mastis, which was answered with a bow and a smile.

The evening passed with a complete recounting of all that Nick and Jazz had experienced since leaving the beaver hut many days before. Nick started with the narration. Jazz interrupted and added more information. Nick jumped in again and continued with the story. Back and forth, heads turned as the animals listened to first one storyteller then the other. As the narration drew near its natural end, Bethany stepped over and sat beside Nick. Taking his hand in hers and looking into his eyes she asked, "May I add something?"

Surprised by the show of both affection and boldness, Nick stammered, "Oh, of course you may, Bethany. After all, this is your story, too."

Bethany, still holding Nick's hand, turned toward the large group of animals that had gathered to hear them recount the events of their travels. They all leaned slightly forward, eager to hear what the infamous kidnap victim was about to say.

She began, "For many years, so many I cannot count, I have been under Hasbadana's control in the Dark Kingdom. He berated me and degraded me. He convinced me that I was of no worth to anyone, including him. I had come to him in such a weakened state of mind and heart that it was not hard for him to convince me of my insignificance. He had even persuaded me that Lady, I mean Shema, had no love in her heart for me." Here she paused and looked over at Shema with a loving sparkle in her eyes. "He cast me off to the darkest corner in his kingdom so he wouldn't have to look at me any longer. There, on the cold, stone floor of my prison, I lay in complete hopelessness. I had no expectation of rescue and had resigned myself to living for the rest of eternity there in that awful tower. In an instant, everything changed in my life. Nicholas and Jazz entered my room and brought their light and love with them. They set immediately to work healing my broken heart and mind, filling me with the power they possess." She turned toward Nick, smiling and squeezing his hand.

Nick felt himself blush and Jazz let out a low nicker of amusement. Nick sent him a look of derision and Jazz looked quickly away with a large smile on his face.

Bethany continued, "By the time Hasbadana arrived, Jazz and Nicholas had filled me with an immense amount of strength. Though I was still physically weak, I had a renewed hope inside of me. I could feel life returning to every cell of my body. I wanted to live. I wanted to be healed. I wanted to become all I have the potential to become. When Hasbadana came into the room, I admit I had to fight off the old fear and dread that he always brought with him. But I turned my focus away from the darkness and kept my attention on the light that Nicholas and Jazz were pouring into me. Now I am safe once again, surrounded by all of you," she looked from one adoring animal to the next and gave each of them a smile.

A cheer went up from the group. Monkeys and birds chirped and chattered in the trees, lions roared, and lambs and goats bleated. Animals of all kinds expressed their joy and excitement at the rescue of a single soul.

At last Mastis arose. Everyone became silent and turned toward the renowned and respected unicorn. "As you have all noticed, I am certain, we have some additional guests with us. As Nicholas and Jazz recounted their story, you heard of the gallant efforts of several dark unicorns to assist them as they tried to escape. I fear that, without their help, Nicholas and Jazz might be telling a far different story in a far different place. I think it is appropriate at this time to hear from their leaders, Salamite and Portlas." Turning toward the two Clydesdales, Mastis addressed them. "Would you share with us what is in your hearts at this time?"

Salamite and Portlas looked at one another. Portlas spoke only to say, "I will let Salamite speak for both of us." Swishing his tail rapidly from side to side, he took a step back, leaving

Salamite to stand alone under the powerful stares of all the animals.

Salamite cleared his throat and shook his mane. "My dear friends, for indeed you are friends to me, it has been a long time since I have been in the light. I was one of the many unicorns that chose to follow Hasbadana when he rebelled against Urijah. I do not excuse myself when I say that Hasbadana is possessed with a great power of persuasion. He is smooth of tongue and I became convinced that he was correct in his assertion that we are the rightful rulers of all the Earth. Soon after being cast out to the Dark Kingdom, Hasbadana appointed Portlas and myself to be his personal guards. We perceived this to be a great honor and took our responsibilities seriously, never leaving his side. As such, I was able to become intimately acquainted with the Lord of the Dark Kingdom. I observed every infinitesimal detail of his behavior and was eventually able to read his true motivation."

Salamite's voice rose in power and volume. "His desire is not to save the Animal Kingdom from unrighteous domination by humans. His desire is to enslave all of us." He looked from one animal to another and to the two humans as well. "His quest is to gain power for himself by controlling the rest of us. Do not, for a moment, question what I say. I have seen his method firsthand. I saw him draw the power from many of the dark unicorns. I saw the techniques he used on Bethany to take what little power she had. And I experienced his evil designs firsthand in the burning, crumbling tower. Only Hasbadana rose above the flames, more powerful than ever, and he did this because he drew the power from all thirteen of his guards who were there to protect him."

Salamite began talking faster and faster. "He drew away our power and left us weak and helpless to be carried down to the bottom of the crater with the rubble. There he abandoned us for eternity, we being of no further use to him."

The other dark unicorns shook their heads, swished their tails, and stomped their hooves in anger and agreement…all except Portlas who stood frozen in place.

The audience didn't take their eyes off Salamite, waiting with bated breath for him to continue. Salamite bowed his head and closed his eyes. He stood silently for several minutes. After taking a few deep breaths, he raised his head and looked into Mastis' eyes. Salamite continued. "For so long Hasbadana taught me that the virtues the unicorns strive to perfect were foolish. In fact, his plan is to go through the mist and first target those noble and great horses who display those very virtues to the utmost degree, thus stopping them in their potential progression toward unicornhood."

He turned his head and looked directly at Nick and Jazz who, like the others, were giving Salamite their rapt attention. "Yet, it is because Master Nicholas and Jazz possess those virtues that I am here today. Think for a moment of the virtues that unicorns are taught: loyalty, cleanliness, intelligence, work, honesty, patience, kindness, courage, dependability and, most of all, love. These are the virtues that, combined, brought Nicholas and Jazz into the Dark Kingdom to save Bethany. These are also the virtues that prompted them to risk their own safety to rescue us from the crater."

Salamite stopped speaking and walked up to Nick and Jazz. All eyes followed his movement. "Master Nicholas and Jazz, you are our saviors. We will serve you for the rest of eternity." The huge dark unicorn bowed, folding his left front leg and dropping his head until his great horn touched the ground. As one, the eleven soldiers did the same. And last of all, Portlas.

~chapter 21~
Decisions

Word of Nick and Jazz's return and the company of unicorns that came with them spread rapidly from the Animal Kingdom to Celestia. Every unicorn and fairy in Celestia was speculating on what the Council of the Twelve Ancients would decide to do with the dark unicorns. No meal was complete without a comprehensive reiteration of the events as they were known. As is typical of any rumor mill, the story became larger and more outlandish with each telling. There were even some rumors spreading throughout the kingdom that Nick had convinced Hasbadana himself to change his ways and return with them back to Celestia.

The Council Chambers buzzed with activity. Mastis had communicated with the Council and kept them informed of the events that had taken place. The animal carvings in the dome of the foyer danced and pranced around excitedly, all except the turtle who just watched and waited patiently. The centurions who ordinarily stood guard at the Council Chambers moved their position to the front of the outer doors. They stood on either side of the enormous gold doors supported by their bejeweled frame and strained their eyes as they watched the horizon for the arrival of their anticipated guests.

Urijah and his counselors met behind closed doors for the better part of the day. Each Council member shared his opinion regarding the arrival of the thirteen dark unicorns. Some held the position that it was extremely dangerous to allow the dark unicorns to return to the Animal Kingdom and that, perhaps, they intended to recruit more converts to their cause. Others held to the belief that even the darkest soul can repent and return to the light and should be embraced and encouraged in their efforts.

After listening to the discussion, which had been heated at times, Urijah rose to his hooves. All dialogue stopped instantly. Heads turned to him, ears pointed straight forward. "My beloved brethren of the Council of the Twelve Ancients," began Urijah, "I have been listening to your carefully thought through opinions on this matter for most of this day. You, as a group of wise advisors, seem to be exceedingly polarized on this issue. Some of you have focused your arguments on the potential danger that the presence of Hasbadana's followers present to all of the unicorns in Celestia. There is no question in my mind that there exists the possibility that Hasbadana desires to infiltrate Celestia with his spies. Along with this is the possibility that he intends for his followers to attempt to persuade additional unicorns to join his crusade. If he is preparing to move forward with his evil designs, he may desire converts to his cause to strengthen his efforts."

At this point, Urijah paused and looked up toward the ceiling for several minutes. Protocol required that his counselors wait patiently for him to continue. Eventually he lowered his eyes and looked around the room at these wise unicorns that he loved so dearly. "Celestia has been created with love and for the purpose of service to all the Animal Kingdom. The greatest measure of our love is reflected in our ability to forgive. Yes, I realize that there is a great risk in forgiveness in that we open ourselves up to the possibility of immense disappointment and pain. However, one lesson I have learned in my long life is that we cannot truly love if we don't take those risks. We must recognize the goodness inherent in all creation, all creatures. That goodness, however dormant, however deeply buried, has the power to rise up within any soul and overcome all evil. Has this inherent goodness done so in these thirteen dark unicorns? I do not know. But it is my decision that we interview them and try to determine the true state of their hearts. If we can read what is in their souls, we will know better what we should do. Let us welcome them with open hearts and hope that their desires are pure."

With this declaration, all the unicorns on both sides of the argument accepted their wise leader's decision, and the Council was reunited. The rainbows of light radiating from the sparkling bodies of the Council danced around the room once more. They opened their council room doors and requested a meal. This was quickly provided by the unicorns in the foyer.

Not long after the Council came to its unified decision, and they were again of one heart and one mind, the centurions at the front doors noticed movement on the edge of the meadow. Both of them stared across the meadow and waited. Within a matter of minutes it became apparent that what had caught their attention was a cluster of unicorns approaching the sculpted turrets of the Council Chambers.

A large faction of fairies arrived ahead of the group of unicorns. "Attention, Attention! Mastis is arriving with his protégées Jazz and Nicholas. They are returning from the Dark Kingdom victorious. Let the notice go out to all," announced the lead fairy Gidoni in his high-pitched voice, made even higher by his excitement.

Junia, who had been flying beside Gidoni, chuckled at her friend's flare for the dramatic, but she, too, was proud of Nick and Jazz's accomplishments. "Perhaps we should mention the dark unicorns…?" she asked Gidoni.

"Oh, yes. And they have brought with them thirteen… how do I put this? Um… guests from the Dark Kingdom," added Gidoni.

The centurions smiled. All of this news had of course already made its way to the Council Chambers and everyone therein eagerly awaited their presence. No matter. They simply bowed and said, "Thank you for the notice. We look forward to their imminent arrival."

Sparkling rays of light bounced in all directions from the bodies of Mastis and Shema as they led their party at a gallop toward the bicolored domes that marked the location of the Council Chambers. They rapidly crossed the meadow. The group came to an abrupt halt in front of the centurions that guarded the gold doors protecting the entrance to the home of the Council of the Ancients and the Lord of Celestia.

"Mastis and company, we have been in eager anticipation of your arrival. Please enter. Urijah and the Council are expecting you." Both unicorns bowed until their horns touched the ground and Mastis and Shema responded in kind.

The gold doors swung open and the entire entourage passed through the jeweled doorway into the enormous foyer. The beautiful mosaic floor shone and reflected the light from their bodies as the sound of their hooves resounded off the walls. The domed ceiling changed from yellow to orange, red to purple. With each change of color, a shower of twinkling stars fell to the tile floor. The carved columns sparkled and reflected the colors of the dome. Beautiful music filled the air. Nick looked up and was surprised to see that only the animal sculptures surrounding the dome seemed subdued as they watched Mastis and his friends lead the dark unicorns toward the doors of the Council Chambers.

The large chestnut unicorns that had been on duty watching for their arrival hurried past the visitors and took their posts in front of the entrance to the Council Chambers. The assemblage stopped in front of the golden doors and waited. The doors remained shut. No one said anything. Nick, sitting on Jazz, and Bethany, sitting atop Shema, exchanged glances.

Do you think we are not welcome? Nick asked Jazz in his thoughts.

Mastis answered Nick's question. "The Council will speak to me first. The rest of you are to wait here." Without looking back, Mastis stepped forward and the doors immediately opened to admit him. Mastis entered the Council Chamber and the doors shut behind him, leaving the little group to wait anxiously.

While they waited in silence, Nick searched the feelings of the others in the group. Each member of the party seemed lost in their own thoughts. Nick opened his mind first to Salamite who stood motionless behind Jazz.

Salamite's thoughts were clear and easy to hear. He had not been in this beautiful building of light since the day he had chosen to follow Hasbadana. His heart ached within him as he rehearsed the events of that day in his mind. He was filled with shame and regret at the choice he had made at that time. He grieved internally for all that had taken place as a result of that decision. Nick felt sympathy well up inside of him for Salamite.

The eleven dark unicorns were thinking about similar memories and their feelings of sadness and regret all seemed to be the same. Nick turned his power toward Portlas. The big bay Clydesdale stood at the back of the group. His head was up and his eyes stared straight ahead. Nick focused his concentration on him in order to hear his thoughts but nothing came into Nick's psyche from Portlas. An invisible wall shielded Portlas' mind from intrusion. Nick could not pick up anything Portlas was thinking or feeling.

What do you make of that? came Jazz's thoughts to Nick. Jazz had been following Nick's mental explorations.

I don't know. Why can't I receive any of Portlas' thoughts? Is his mind closed to thinking and feeling, or just closed to me?

It is my guess that Portlas has developed the ability to block visitors to his mind. I had heard that was possible, though it must be a difficult skill to master, responded Jazz.

Nick wondered about this for a time, but eventually turned his attention to Bethany. She sat on Shema's back, stroking her mane as she thought about her childhood adventures with the mare she loved. A smile caressed her face. Nick felt his cheeks blush as he heard her thoughts turn to him. *Perhaps this ability will come in handy when it comes to understanding the opposite sex,* he said in his thoughts to Jazz.

Jazz responded with a snort and a shake of his head.

Without warning, the Council Chamber doors opened and Mastis stepped out. "My dear brothers from the Dark Kingdom, Urijah and the Council of the Twelve Ancients would like to speak with you first." He stepped aside and gave a slight movement with his head to indicate that the time had come for them to enter. The thirteen dark unicorns, led by Salamite, walked past Jazz and Shema. Portlas brought up the rear of the line. He turned to look at Nick as he walked by. For a moment, their eyes met, but Nick was unable to read his expression. He gave Nick a slight nod, turned his head forward and self-assuredly walked into the chambers.

Mastis looked toward Nick and gave him a wink of his eye before following the rest of the unicorns into the room. The doors shut behind them, leaving Nick, Jazz, Shema, and Bethany to wait and wonder.

Nick extended the power of his thoughts toward the doors in an attempt to connect with Salamite or one of the other unicorns. Nothing. He felt the same barrier he felt when he tried to reach Portlas. *Perhaps the doors have been given the power to block your thoughts. Logic dictates that the Council needs that kind of privacy on occasion*, thought Jazz in response to Nick's efforts.

I guess you are right, Jazz. I should have thought of that. Nick turned to Shema and Bethany. Remembering that Bethany had not developed the power to communicate with her thoughts, he spoke aloud, his voice mingling with the music that floated on the air. "How are you feeling, Bethany?"

She turned to look at him with softness in her eyes that spread across her facial features. She had never looked so beautiful. "I am home," she said with a smile as she rubbed Shema's neck. Nick smiled back at her and a warm current flowed through his body.

Behind the gold doors, Urijah and his Council stood to greet the dark unicorns. One by one, Hasbadana's traitors lined up abreast with one another, facing the Council of the Ancients, the same group that had cast them out long ago. Twelve of the heads were held low, eyes cast to the floor. Only Portlas stood with his head up, eyes looking straight ahead. Salamite gained his composure and cleared his throat. He looked at his companions, who stood on both sides of him. They all bowed. Urijah and the Council acknowledged their greeting in kind.

Urijah spoke first. "My dear brethren, our hearts are filled with joy as we welcome you back to Celestia. Mastis," and he acknowledged the beautiful glowing dapple-gray unicorn that stood to the side of the room where he could observe the proceedings, "has told us of your courage and sacrifice. We are indebted to you for helping Nicholas and Jazz rescue Bethany."

Urijah paused and looked from one unicorn soldier to the next. He paused at each one, carefully studying their demeanor. He smiled when he came to Salamite. "Salamite, my heart is filled with love for you. I remember well the time we spent together here in Celestia. Hasbadana was a wonderful teacher for you in those days and I had great hopes for you. Your actions these past few days tell me that I was not wrong about you. There is greatness in you that can be used for good."

Salamite dropped his eyes to conceal the tears that were welling up in them. Urijah's eyes moved on to each of the remaining unicorns. The Lord of Celestia called each of them by name and shared kind words of welcome for each of them.

Finally, his examination rested upon Portlas. "Ah, my son, Portlas. Welcome back."

Portlas, whose head had been up, dropped his gaze until he met Urijah's. He said nothing, his face expressionless. Mastis looked from one to the other. The silence was uncomfortable, yet no unicorn dared to speak.

When Urijah spoke at last, everyone breathed a little easier. Addressing the entire group he said, "The Council has met for several hours concerning the matter of your return. As you know, we have never before been faced with a decision such as this. While it is a happy matter to discuss, we desire to make the best decision for everyone involved. After much careful consideration, we have decided to allow you to remain in Celestia under a period of probation. If you prove that you have truly repented of your sins, all of your previous powers will, one day, be returned to you."

A high level of excitement filled the room as the dark unicorns looked up in disbelief at what they were hearing. This was far beyond any of their expectations. Portlas turned his huge head toward Salamite and the two exchanged enormous smiles.

Mastis could hear what Salamite was thinking but Portlas' thoughts were blocked to him. Mastis was touched, however, by the humility Salamite was expressing in his thoughts. The massive bay Clydesdale unicorn was stunned that such forgiveness was being offered to him and his companions. The love being extended to them was so potent that it brought him to tears. He had not felt such light and power for so long that he had forgotten the intense beauty of love. Mastis hoped that Portlas was of the same sentiment.

Urijah spoke once more. "My dear friends, we, the Lord and Council of Celestia, desire to give each of you our blessing."

One by one, the thirteen dark unicorns stepped forward. Urijah and Helam, followed by each of the other Council members, stepped forward as well and stopped first in front of Salamite. They leaned down and touched the dark unicorn's right shoulder, then his left shoulder, then the tip of his horn. They repeated this in front of each of the dark unicorns. As each Council member completed a blessing, the darkness began to subside from Hasbadana's soldiers. Their eyes softened, the angles of their bodies seemed to round out and go from sharp to smooth. The coldness that had filled them was replaced with warmth. Their bodies did not sparkle and exude light as they had at one time, but they were clearly not the creatures who, a short time earlier, had so timidly entered the room. The fear and trepidation was gone from each heart; the seed of love had been planted again.

Nick, Jazz, Bethany, and Shema stepped back, mouths agape when the doors to the Council Chamber opened and the little band of unicorns walked toward them. The change in both their appearance and demeanor was immediately obvious. Jazz and Nick understood immediately what that meant. "You are staying with us in Celestia," said Nick with excitement.

All of the unicorns, even Portlas, answered at once with their own version of what had taken place behind the closed doors. Exhilaration filled the air as the story was told. Unicorns from all over the palace stopped to listen. Even the dancing statues in the dome stopped their movement to observe what was occurring below them. The dome ceiling sent down stars of all different colors at once in recognition of the joyous occasion. This was a first for Celestia, the return of some of Hasbadana's followers, and everyone knew what a historic event it was.

No one noticed when the Chamber doors opened once more. Mastis stood smiling as he watched the celebratory words and actions of each of the unicorns and the two humans that were taking place in the great hall. The beautiful dapple-gray unicorn turned his attention to Nick. Nick heard the kind, gentle words in his mind. *Nicholas, bring Jazz, Bethany, and Shema. The Council is ready to speak with you.*

Nick looked up, startled at the suddenness of the instructions he received. For a moment, he had forgotten that he, too, would be meeting with the Council. Jazz had heard the message as well and turned his head to look back at Nick. "Bethany, we have been summoned," said Nick.

Bethany, who had been laughing with delight as the restored unicorns took turns telling their stories, stopped and looked at Nick. She nodded and slid off of Shema's back.

Nick also slid to the floor, stepped over to Bethany and took her hand. He resolutely turned toward the golden doors that stood open and waiting for them and walked forward. Jazz and Shema followed behind. The gathering of unicorns ceased their celebration and became silent as they watched their four newly beloved friends enter the Council Chamber. The doors shut once again.

Urijah and his counselors were arranged in their customary semicircle. Nick and Bethany blinked their eyes several times to adjust to the brightness of the Council's glowing bodies. Sparkling, multicolored rays of light danced around the room. All was aglow; all was warm. Joy filled Nick's heart as he looked at Urijah, who stood in the front of the room and smiled down at him. Jazz stepped up beside Nick, and Shema stepped up beside Bethany. Nick squeezed Bethany's hand tightly as they stood before this Council of wise rulers.

"Welcome back, Nicholas, Jazz, and Bethany," began Urijah. "We are both relieved and delighted by your safe return and successful mission. As a result, I would like to get right to the point of this audience." He turned his attention to Jazz. "Jazz, it is my pleasure to inform you that, by unanimous approval of the Council, you have been deemed worthy to become a member of the Legion of the Unicorn and receive your horn."

Nick let go of Bethany's hand and threw his arms around Jazz's neck. "Oh, Jazz! That is such wonderful news. Congratulations!" Bethany, too, was at his side, stroking the silky dark coat that glistened in the light of the room. The entire Council beamed with approving smiles, but none could match the sparkling glow coming from Mastis.

"Well, what do you say to that?" asked Urijah kindly, his smile impossible to conceal.

"I am honored and humbled, Lord Urijah. I thank all of you for the confidence you have placed in me, but I have done nothing on my own. Nicholas has been beside me each step of the way."

"Yes," responded Urijah. "We are all aware of the enormity of Nicholas's contributions and we stand in awe at the greatness of his soul. As a result, we have concurred as a Council that it seems only appropriate that both of you become members of the Legion of the Unicorn. If he so chooses, Nicholas will become the first unicorn rider in Celestia." Nick heard a gasp escape from Shema, but he couldn't take his eyes off of Urijah to turn to look at her, as though Urijah had him under a spell, a spell cast by the power of love.

Urijah continued, "As recipients of this highest of all appointments in Celestia, you will be responsible to become saviors in the Animal Kingdom. You will be required to travel through the mist when called upon to bring an animal from their earthly life to their immortal life. If the animal is a noble and great horse, you might be assigned to be his or her instructor to prepare them to become unicorns and earn their horns as Mastis has done for you."

Nick, still holding onto Jazz's neck, yet still under Urijah's spell, continued staring at the magnificent Lord of Celestia, stunned by the immensity of the message he was hearing.

Focusing on Nick, Urijah continued. "Nicholas, I want you to understand that this is the first time in all eternity that the Legion of the Unicorn has accepted a human into its ranks. This is not only a tremendous honor, but a unique responsibility. Membership in this organization requires, however, an important decision on your part. If you choose to be inducted into the Legion, you will have to commit to spending all of eternity as part of the Animal Kingdom." He paused.

Nick was about to jump in with an enthusiastic acceptance when Urijah held up a hoof to stop him. "Before you make your decision, there are some guests here to see you."

All heads turned as one toward an archway on the side of the room. Nick followed their gaze and felt himself fall to his knees. Walking toward him was his family: his mother, his father, his little sisters and, bouncing enthusiastically beside them all, Belle, his beloved poodle.

His mother reached him first and knelt in front of him, throwing her arms around him. She sobbed so hard that her entire body shook, but no harder than Nick's. In less than a second, his father and sisters had joined their embrace and the entire family hugged and cried as one, together at last. Belle hopped around the tight circle, on her hind legs, until Nick reached out, brought her to him, and gave her a warm hug.

Bethany, Jazz, and the unicorns stood silently watching, not wanting to interrupt this sacred family reunion. A great sense of longing filled Bethany's heart and she reached over and interlocked her fingers in Shema's glowing white mane. The mare turned her head and nuzzled Bethany's cheek. Bethany reached up with her other hand and stroked Shema's face.

When the family had shed their tears, they looked around at one another and started giggling and laughing. Nick's excitement started spilling out of him. "Mom! Dad! Nancy! Lynn! Belle! I didn't know if I would ever see you again. Mastis told me that perhaps I would have the chance and I hung on to that hope. And now here you are…in Celestia! This is too good to be true." He paused to take a breath before he continued, "Oh, yes, pardon me. Have you met my friends?"

He turned toward Mastis, who had stepped up beside Shema. Motioning toward Mastis, Nick said, "This is Mastis, he brought Jazz and me to the land behind the mist. He has been our teacher while we have been in Celestia. And this is Shema. She helped to heal us. And this is Bethany, the only other human to have been brought to Celestia. Shema brought her, just like Jazz brought me."

Then, addressing his friends, "This is my family, my mom, Jeannie, my dad, Tom, and my little sisters, Lynn and Nancy." With a sweeping motion of his arm he acknowledged the Council. "And this is the Council of the Twelve Ancients and the Lord of Celestia, Urijah."

"Yes," said his father with a warm smile, "we have met them."

"Oh, yes, of course you have," said Nick with a blush.

"Now, my son," said his father, a serious tone now creeping into both his voice and the expression on his face, "for you will always be my son, the Council has told us of the wonderful work you have been doing, of the powers you have developed, and the success you have had going into the Dark Kingdom."

"I wasn't pleased to hear that you did that," interrupted his mother. She could not conceal the pride in her voice even with her attempt to look stern.

"I thought it sounded awesome!" interjected Nancy.

"Me, too," added Lynn.

Nick turned to look at them. "It wasn't awesome; it was terrible," he said solemnly. He leaned over and gave each of his sisters a hug before turning back to his father.

"Yes, well, you have done a wonderful act of service by rescuing Bethany. I know she will be eternally grateful," he said while looking over his head at the lovely young girl standing silently beside Shema. Bethany was leaning against her unicorn's shoulder for support. She smiled warmly at Nick's father in acknowledgement.

"The Council has also told us of the offer they have made to you to stay and serve in the Animal Kingdom." At this, his mother dropped her head and began to weep and Tom put his arm tightly around her shoulder. Belle stepped over to Jeannie and pressed her head against her leg to comfort her.

Tom continued, "You must make a decision where you would like to spend your immortality. Do you desire to stay here and serve the animals or would you like to come with us to the human kingdom and join us in our labors there?"

Nick sat back on his heels. "Mom, Dad, if staying in Celestia means that I could never see you again, then I will leave with you this instant...but..." and he turned to Urijah with pleading in his eyes. Still speaking to his family but beseeching Urijah, he said, "If I would be able to visit you frequently, then I would choose to stay and serve the animals and fight against Hasbadana and his evil campaign. I would choose to be a member of the Legion of the Unicorn."

Everyone turned to look at Urijah and waited. Urijah returned Nick's stare for a long time. A warm smile crossed his face and he nodded. Cheers erupted all around the room. Tom clapped his son on the back; Lynn and Nancy hugged and kissed their brother; Jeannie cried. Nick took his mother in his arms and they both cried and laughed together.

Belle jumped up, placed her front legs around Nick's hips and pressed her head against his chest. "Don't forget about me," said the curly white poodle. Nick stroked her long, fluffy ears.

"Don't worry, I will visit you, too, Belle," he said with a laugh. He shook his head in wonderment. How things had changed since he had been in Celestia. Speaking with the animals was second nature to him now and he was grateful for this gift.

Nick eventually disentangled himself from his family's embrace and walked over to Bethany. He stood in front of her for a moment. She stared into his face, searching his eyes. He reached down and took both of her hands in his. Without taking his eyes from Bethany, he spoke over his shoulder. "Urijah, there is one other thing I would like."

"Yes, my son, what would that be?"

"I would like Bethany, if she so chooses, to stay here with me."

Bethany let out a quiet whimper and threw her arms around Nick. Burying her head against his chest, she sobbed. Nick wrapped one arm around her and stroked her hair with the other hand. "I love you, Bethany," he whispered "I have loved you since the first night I saw you."

Bethany leaned back, her face turned up toward Nick's. Her eyes were gently closed, her cheeks wet with tears. But her mouth formed a smile that seemed to reach beyond the confines of her face as she let his words wash over her like a warm mist.

The Mist Continues
Look for the next book in The Mist Trilogy:

Mists of Darkness

Available soon wherever fine books are sold

Visit the *Behind the Mist* website:
www.behindthemist.com

Join the conversation at:
themisttrilogy.blogspot.com

About the Author

M.J. Evans is a graduate of Oregon State University and a lifelong equestrian. She is a former teacher at the secondary school level. She and her husband are the parents of five children and live in Colorado with their three horses and a Standard Poodle.